EMMA LOUISE

Edited by Jenn Wood at All About The Edits

Cover Designed by Mary Ruth at Passion Creations

Formatting by Silla Webb at Masque of the Red Pen

To Adriana.

Thank you for turning a dream into reality.

Sometimes, two people have to fall apart

to realize how much they need to fall back together

-unknown

Prologue

10 years ago

"Baby girl, you know we're going to be fine, right?"

His whisper is rough in my ear, his breath heavy against my skin, and it sends a shiver racing through me. We've been here, in his bed, for most of the day. Anytime he unwinds his body from mine, a cold strike of fear rushes through me. Right now, he's pressed up against my back, his arms wrapped around my chest, his chin propped on my shoulder. I let my eyes trail around the room. The TV is still on; the abandoned movie has long since ended and the screen plays ads for God knows what useless crap. There are clothes strewn around and you can see how our passionate greeting this morning has played out by how far and wide our clothes are dispersed.

An old hoodie of mine is hanging on the back of the door, mixed in with his jackets. I can't see them, but I know that I have a drawer full of clothes in that dresser over there and my toothbrush is next to his in the bathroom next door. There's a small glass bowl on the bedside table next to me that holds my loose change and hair ties. It's right there, on my side of his bed.

When I take too long to reply, he lets out a deep sigh. "You don't need to worry. I promise."

I can hear in his voice how much he needs me to believe what he's saying. Trying my hardest to hide how scared I am, I turn onto my back to gaze up at him. My arms snake up his broad shoulders, and I run my fingers up into the hair at the nape of his neck, pulling him down on top of me. Even the smallest of distances between us is unbearable right now. I wish I could lay here forever, with our naked bodies pressed together, reveling in the feeling of his hard body against my much softer one.

"I'm sorry," I finally manage to say. "I hate being this insecure, but have you seen you?" I try to make light of my bad attitude, but I can still hear the pout in my own voice. I can't help it. He lets out a small laugh and squeezes me closer, settling us on our sides, face to face.

"It's just a few months, baby. Not even a year. Think of all the peace you'll have, to study without me groping you all the time." That pulls another small smile from me as he continues to speak quietly. "And by the time you're done with school, I'll be settled, I'll have a place for us to live. You can look for a job, if that's what you really want."

God, I love this man. I love how strong he's being right now while I'm falling apart. "You know we'll be able to talk every day, and you can come up and see me whenever you want."

Rolling me to my back again, he props himself over me on his elbows. As his lips pepper mine with kisses, he keeps talking. “Just say the word and I’ll take you with me. We’ll find you classes at another school. I’ll do whatever makes you happy.”

As tempting as that sounds right now, we both know it won’t happen. I’ll be here in school and he’ll be in Seattle, playing football and living the high life. Traveling and parties, with groupies and more money than he’ll know what to do with. Just thinking of it fills me with dread.

He must sense the rising panic because before I know what’s happening, his kisses become more forceful, like he’s trying to brand his promises right there on my lips. Once he feels me melt into him, he gently pulls away, so he can stare into my eyes again.

“I swear to you, I don't want to leave you, but this is a good thing for us in the long run. We’ll have everything we’ve ever wanted. Together. I’m going pro, baby.”

This is what makes me feel like the biggest bitch ever. This is his dream and I know I’m acting like a brat, but I can’t help it. I hate how happy he sounds. Why can’t I at least *try* to act like I’m ok? I know he’s right. I’ve known this was his dream from the day I met him almost a year ago. He’d told me that first night, the night I’d gotten up on stage with my drunk friends and sang a song I can't even remember the name of now.

When I’d looked out through the lights at the crowd, and saw Keir looking right back at me.

One drink turned into two that night, and that turned into a first date a week later. I might have only just turned twenty and had little experience with men, but I knew enough to know that he was special. That *we* had that something special.

Even though he'd been honest and told me that if everything went as planned, he wouldn't be here for long, it still didn't stop me from falling head over heels in love with him. So now, here we are. Me, with a year of school left, and him being a draft pick for an NFL team, two thousand miles away.

Laying here in his bed with him, watching the shadows crawl over the walls as the sun sets, it's easy to believe him when he says we would be ok. When he whispers words of love and promises of a future with me, I could almost silence the voice telling me this was goodbye.

With my head cradled in his safe hands, I let him kiss some of my fears away. I let him brush more of them aside with each sweep of his hands over my body. Every inch of my skin he loves helps his words take root. And as he finally sinks inside me, I let those fears go.

What a fool I was.

One

Poppy

Present

"Oh my. This place looks spectacular," my best friend murmurs quietly from beside me, her eyes wide as she gazes around the huge room we just entered. She's right. The usually bland hotel conference room has been transformed into something quite stunning. The bare walls have been draped in shimmering fabric with twinkling lights throughout. There are three separate bar areas placed around the huge space, and various stations set up with blackjack and roulette tables. The dining tables are dressed with black and gold covers, and the tall table displays are draped in long strings of shiny black beads.

The room screams opulence.

"It sure does. I'm glad you forced me to wear this dress now," I say, running a hand down the full skirt of my black dress. I wasn't sure if the long-sleeved lace dress would be too formal. The full tutu-style skirt hits mid-calf and makes it a little more fun than a full evening gown. Elliott, my best friend, had arrived at my door with it a few hours ago, and practically forced me into it.

“Poppy!”

Turning at the sound of my name being called, I see one of my clients, Kate, dragging her husband, Billy, over to us. “Thank you so much for coming,” she says, pulling me in for a brief hug and kiss to my cheek.

“Thank you for the invite,” I reply, giving her a small squeeze back.

“Of course. We can’t thank you enough for all of your help. An invite is the least we can do,” Billy says, as he takes his turn giving me a hug.

Kate and I met in college, and when she and Billy later decided to set up their own business after graduation, they had asked me to do their websites. When they needed help creating one for their new children’s charity, I’d offered my services for free.

“It was nothing.” I can't help the blush that heats my cheeks, and I have to fight the urge to shy away from the compliment.

“Billy and I have to go greet some more people, but please, get yourselves a drink and take a look at the silent auction items. We’ve had some amazing donations,” Kate says before they turn and head in the direction of the streams of people coming in.

“There is some serious talent here tonight.” Elliott looks around in awe, and she’s not wrong. It’s like a beautiful people convention. Her eyes stop on a group of guys standing around the bar. “Holy shit. I’d climb him like a tree,” she whispers loudly, leering at a lumberjack-in-a-tux type.

“I can’t take you anywhere,” I say, looking around to make sure no one else heard her.

“I said he was hot. I didn’t lick him, for crying out loud. Although...” She trails off, and I shake my head. She’s so full of it.

"You do know you’re married, right?" I reply, making us both laugh. Elliott has been married to her college sweetheart for years.

“Married. Not dead, Pop. Come on. There’s a couple of wine glasses over there with our names on them.” She drags me toward the bar as fast as my heels will allow.

Taking a large gulp of my wine, I try to will myself into relaxing some. This is the first time I’ve been out anywhere, other than a few restaurants, since I’ve been back in Savannah. When I’d finished college ten years ago, I’d taken my degree and my broken heart, and accepted the first job offer that would get me far, far away from here.

I didn’t care that I’d been running away. There was no way I would have been able to stay here. The looks from the other students on campus, along with the whispers and snide commentary that followed me everywhere, were dragging me down. I was *that girl.* The one that everyone had been waiting to see fall, and they had loved every second of my misery when it had happened. If I hadn't moved away, I would have drowned under the weight of their scrutiny.

Despite all that, I still missed living here. I'd grown up a few hours outside of Savannah and after spending summers here with my grandparents, I'd fallen in love with the city. Although I'd gotten offers from colleges all over the U.S., I decided to stay here. The mix of history, and that certain magical vibe only Savannah has, had gotten under my skin. No matter where I lived after college, nowhere was like Savannah, Georgia.

That didn't mean I hadn't tried to make a life elsewhere. I had friends in cities from one side of the U.S. to the other. I'd made real friendships and even tried out a relationship a time or two. No matter what, I still felt a void that I'd tried to fill by working crazy long hours.

When that didn't work, I'd even gotten a dog from a rescue center, thinking he would be a reason to come home from the office before nine p.m. every night. No matter what I did, I always felt like I was missing out on something. When I'd started up my own web design business, I'd realized I could do that from anywhere. So, I'd pulled my head out of my ass, taken a chance, and moved back here.

"Some of these prizes are insane," Elliott says, as we meander along the tables that stretch the whole back wall of the massive room, pulling me from my thoughts.

"A weekend in Vegas, flights on a private jet." She stops in front of another display for a weekend in Maui, letting out a low whistle from between her teeth. "I'm bidding on this. If I win, you can watch the kids for us." She smirks at me.

"Judging by these bids, there is no chance of that happening," I scoff, noticing some of the items are already up to tens of thousands of dollars.

"You have to be in it to win, doll." She writes down a bid I know will make her husband, Pete, cry if she actually wins.

Continuing down the line, I pass more trips, and glass cases full of signed baseballs, jerseys, and cleats. There are a few footballs and a helmet I pass without even glancing at.

I'm *not* a football fan.

As it's a charity night, I try to find something I can bid on without breaking the bank. I find a few items I'd like to try. There's a wine-tasting day that sounds fun, as well as a year membership at the fancy new gym that opened up recently. There's also a signed photo of the latest movie star that every woman I know is half in love with, so I leave a few bids.

By the time we've made it around all the auction items, dinner is about to be served. Once we finally find our table, most of the seats are filled. An elderly couple is seated opposite me with a middle-aged man next to them. The two seats between he and I are empty, and I assume his date will be filling it shortly.

After polite nods to our table companions, we settle into our seats as the waiters bring around the wine and Elliott strikes up a conversation with the lady next to her.

This is why I bring her to any function that requires interaction with other people. I suck at small talk, but she could make it an Olympic event. Barely a minute later, she's already got her phone out, showing off pictures of her kids.

Letting my eyes wander around the room, I see Kate make her way up to the stage. She stops and gives Billy a kiss on the cheek and he gives her belly a small rub before she continues on her way. I guess I'll be getting another baby announcement in my emails soon then. I can't deny the small pang of envy I feel. I never thought I'd be approaching thirty, single and childless.

Keeping up my people-watching, I see a guy walking in the direction of our table. He's tall and classically good-looking, his body filling out his tuxedo very nicely. Slicked back dirty blond hair and a cocky smile plays on his lips. I catch his eye and he gives me a wide smile as he makes his way over.

Placing his hands on the back of the chair next to me, he leans in and asks, "Is this seat taken?"

His voice is softer than I expected. It somehow doesn't quite fit with the face it's coming out of.

"Oh, I'm not sure. We just sat here," I reply with a smile, trying to be friendly. He quickly glances around the table with a raised eyebrow. The gentleman sitting alone gives a quick head shake before returning to his conversation with someone at the next table. After getting the all-clear, he pulls out his chair and subtly moves it closer to me as he sits.

I clear my throat, trying to get Elliott's attention, then offer him a small smile before turning away from him slightly. I can't put my finger on why, but this guy makes me feel uncomfortable. There's a lecherous gleam in his eyes; the way he's looking at me makes my skin crawl. He leans in again, obviously not one for social cues. Holding out his hand for me to take, he speaks again.

"Darren, pleased to meet you…?" He trails off, waiting for me to provide my name.

Feigning politeness, I quickly shake his cold fingers before pulling my hand away. "Nice to meet you, my name is—"

"Her name is Poppy, and you're in my seat."

The deep voice rumbles over my shoulder, making my heart stutter in my chest. I'm frozen in place, too scared to move. If I turn around and see him, it's real.

The guy who broke my heart ten years ago will really be standing behind me.

The sounds of the room fade to nothing; all I can hear is my own heartbeat thundering in my ears. I don't notice him move, but Darren must leave the table because the next thing I know, *he* is next to me. Standing so close, I could easily touch him. My gaze moves from the table in front of me to his broad chest, then to the wonderfully wide shoulders that look even more impressive than they used to be. They continue up the column of a beautiful, tanned throat and pass full lips on a face that's about a week past needing a shave. Finally, they stop on chocolate brown eyes that I once knew better than I knew my own.

Keir Harmon.

Keir

Past

"Here ya go, sugar."

Making sure to lean in nice and low, so I can get a good look at what she's offering—exactly the same move she's pulled the last four times she's gotten me a drink—the bartender places a shot on the sticky bar in front of me. Or is it two shots? I'm past the point of knowing whether or not I'm seeing double. Hoping for the best, I pick up the glass that's moving the least. Who fucking cares anymore?

Not me.

The loud music of the bar thumps through the room, the bass vibrating through my feet. The images that were seared into my brain a few short hours ago throb in and out of my consciousness, in time with the shitty dance track playing. This place is a dive. It suits my mood perfectly.

Lifting the small glass up to my lips, I shoot it straight back, hoping I'll soon be too numb to feel any more of the gutting pain I've been in for the last few hours.

The meaty hand that clamps down on my shoulder causes me to wobble on the bar stool. Luckily, I'm grabbed before I can hit the floor.

"I'm not in the mood for babysitting tonight, man, give it a rest." My roommate, Kyle, yanks the glass out of my hand and pushes it back to the bartender who has been hovering around me for the last hour.

"Fuck off."

"I'm all for drowning your sorrows, but you don't even know if you have any to drown yet. Just call the girl and ask her what the fuck is going on."

He's been saying this since he found me kicking my shattered phone earlier. I can't call her. I can't hear her denials. I saw that picture, and now I'll never be able to forget it. I know I've been a shit boyfriend, but this? I just can't get my head around this. Seeing her in those pictures.

My Poppy. Her arms around some guy, face buried in his chest. She looked fucking beautiful. She looked peaceful, something I've not been able to see on her face for too long. The smile on her face. That fucking smile. The jab to my chest has me reaching out to ask for another drink, but Kyle has other ideas. He's got me up on my feet before I know what's happening.

"Come on. Let's walk it off."

Shrugging him off, I sit back down and raise my chin to get my glass back, and for the bartender to fill it.

"I said, fuck off. If you want to go, go."

"You're making a mistake, Keir. If you want to fuck up, at least do it at home, where no one will see it." His eyes flick to the bartender still hovering. "You know Daniels will kick your ass in training if he finds out you've been getting wrecked the night before."

That almost makes me think about going home.

Almost.

Daniels is one of our trainers, and he's a sadistic bastard when he thinks anyone has turned up to practice hungover.

"Fuck Daniels, and fuck you."

Yeah, I'm not the most mature when I've had a drink, obviously.

Yanking on his hair in frustration, he tries one last time to get me to see sense. "Come on. I'll stop off and get some booze. You can do this at home."

If I go home, I'll call her.

Beg her to pick me over this other guy.

I'm weak for her.

I need to stay here.

Stay where I won't be tempted.

I need to be numb.

In fact, no, I need to get angry. I need to man the fuck up and stop whining over a chick that barely even let my side of the bed get cold before she had someone else in it.

"Last time I'll tell you, man. Back. Off. I'm not interested in your help."

With a shrug of his shoulders, and a look on his face that tells me he thinks I'm pathetic, he leaves. Not a minute later, I'm signaling for another drink, with a twenty in my hand.

Now it's just me and my new best friends, Whiskey and Revenge.

With one eye closed, I try, and fail miserably, to get the key in the door for the fifth time. Why does it keep moving? The body pressed close to my side takes the key from my hand and unlocks the door. Stumbling my way in, I crash into the coffee table before landing on my back on the sofa. The room is spinning so out of control, I have to plant one foot on the ground to try and slow it down.

I'm on the brink of passing out when I feel my boots being pulled off. The room is dark with only thin slivers of moonlight peeking in. The faceless figure that helped me in slowly crawls up from my now shoeless feet until it's straddling my waist, hands at my belt buckle.

Warm kisses start at my neck and travel to my mouth. The tongue that dips in to touch mine feels wrong. Tastes wrong. But unfortunately for me, Whiskey and Revenge don't agree.

The sound of the door slamming shut is like a bomb detonating in my head. Shifting onto my side, I almost roll off the small sofa. Why the hell am I sleeping out here? And why does it feel like something died in my mouth last night? Sitting upright is a huge effort and it takes a minute for the room to stop spinning once I'm vertical.

"Well, well, well. Look who finally woke up."

Is he being that loud on purpose?

"Shut up, man. My head is a mess. What time did we get in?" My voice sounds like I've been chewing gravel all night.

"I got in at nine thirty. You and your 'friend' decided to show up about three a.m. Nice performance, by the way. Maybe next time you can keep that shit in your room, though?"

The sarcasm drips from his words, and I don't need to ask what he's talking about. The memories have already started to flood my brain.

The bartender all over me. Asking if she could come back here. Flashes of whiskey shots. Her lips on mine.

Fuck.

“She just left, by the way. Her number is over there if you want to go again. Her words, not mine.”

My stomach roils, and I don't even know if I’m going to make to the toilet before the shame comes spewing out of me. It doesn’t matter what Poppy did. Just the thought of touching someone else has me drowning in guilt. I wonder if she felt like this after the guy from that photo left her apartment.

“We have training in an hour, man. You need a shower. You stink of regret right now,” Kyle says over his shoulder before he walks out of the apartment. Slamming the door again.

Letting my head drop into my hands, I yank on my hair, my head swimming with thoughts of last night.

Before I can drag myself into the shower, a knock sounds at the door to the apartment. Grabbing my jeans from the floor, I slide them on, leaving the top buttons open. When the door swings open, revealing Poppy standing there, all the air leaves my body.

She’s here. And she’s not alone. Chapter 3

Three

Keir

Present

Poppy Nash.

Just thinking her name causes my chest to tighten in pain. The mental image of her rushing away from me last night, mixed in with memories of how things ended with us before, is torturing me.

When I'd arrived late to the charity event last night, the very last thing I'd expected was to see her again after ten long years.

The one that got away.

The one whose heart I broke, all because of my stupid ego.

Instead of going straight to my seat, I'd stopped at the bar to get a shot to try and help me relax. I hated going to those things, especially when it required wearing a pain-in-the-ass tuxedo. I'd stood there, mentally preparing for a night of boring small talk with a table full of self-important idiots that usually came to these things just to show off just how much they could drop on the auction lots.

Of course, I saw the two blondes pass me as they walked to their table, especially the smaller of the two. It was impossible not to notice the incredible body showcased in black lace. Her hair was swept up in a mess on her head, showing off skin that looked like the smoothest silk. Tight calves peeked out the bottom of the dress, ending with shoes I could easily imagine up around my ears.

It wasn't until she sat down and looked around the room that I finally got a good look at her face. The face that has haunted most of my dreams for the last ten years. The face that's given me sleepless nights because I was drowning in guilt over what I did to her.

My Poppy.

All of the air evaporated from that room. She was all I could see. All I *wanted* to see. For a minute, I'd thought I was imagining her. So many times over the years, I'd thought I'd seen her. In the seats at one of my games, in a bar, on the street.

But it never was.

Although the last time I'd seen her she been a brunette, she still took my breath away with her beauty. No matter where I went or who I was with, I'd never seen a face anywhere near as stunning as hers. She was still just as beautiful, but time had been more than kind to her. She'd grown into her body, and the cute, shy girl I had known before, was now a knockout with curves for days.

I'd intended to walk out without letting her see me. We'd never managed to resolve things all those years ago. That was probably for the best, seeing as I was pretty much full of alcohol and anger those first few months. It was clear to me she was done, and I hated the thought of dragging all that up again for her now.

Before I could move to leave, sneak out without upsetting her, I'd seen that idiot approach her and sit down. Anyone who knew a thing about Poppy would be able to tell how uncomfortable he made her. The tight set of her shoulders and the way she tried to be subtle as she moved her chair closer to Elliott were a dead giveaway. I'd been halfway to the table before I realized what I was doing. The need to protect her was just as strong as it had always been.

Remembering how she had stared at me, stunned into silence for a minute when I'd spoken from behind her, before she made her excuses and left, makes my gut twist and bile start to creep up. After those first few seconds, where she had stared at me in dismay, she'd shut down. Despite wanting to drag her closer to me, I'd let her leave. My hands had begged to reach out and stop her. What right did I have to try and make her stay? To make her talk to me?

She didn't even look at me as she swept up her small bag and ran from the room. Elliott had looked at me like she was seeing a ghost. And I suppose she was. Ten years is a long time. Obviously just not enough to assuage any of the pain I'd caused.

Shouts from outside bring me out of my thoughts of the past. Letting my head drop back against my chair, I blow out a long, deep breath. My head is a mess and I need to get a grip on myself. Moving away from my desk, I stop in the doorway to my office and look out at the huge space in front of me. My brother is in the ring with one of the fighters he's training; this is why he wanted to open this place. Seeing how passionate he is about what he does made it an easy decision to invest, even if he is a little unconventional at times.

"Dude, are you on your fucking period or what?" my brother yells as he bobs and weaves his way around the ring, hands up, protecting his pretty boy face. The guy he's sparring with is losing his shit at the taunts my brother is throwing his way.

"Jab, jab, punch. That's it! Keep it up! Come on!" TJ keeps yelling loudly, being as obnoxious as he can be.

"Suck my fat dick," the guy wheezes out, obviously getting tired now.

They keep going for another ten minutes, with insults flying back and forth. Standing in the doorway to my office, I look around the basement of the gym TJ and I opened nearly two years ago. The space is huge, with a boxing ring and a few speedbags down here. Upstairs has the main weight and training room, and a few studios for various classes we offer. I love hearing the bass from the up-tempo music thrumming through the ceiling, and the bangs and rattles of the machinery. It's music to my ears.

Did I expect to be here at this time in my life? Hell no. At thirty-two, I thought I'd still be flying high in the NFL. I'd been drafted after college and after a disastrous year stint in Seattle, I'd been traded to LA. It was a miracle they took me on. I was a mess.

My first year in the pros was a blur of football, parties, and drinking. I'd come so close to losing my spot on the team, and after a particularly fucked-up weekend, the GM told me Seattle had had enough. I was out. Luckily, the LA Sharks took a chance, and I eventually turned my life around some. I stayed there until a cleat to the knee ended my dream at just twenty-nine.

I don't even know if I miss it anymore. I miss the thrill of being out there on the field. I don't miss the mess it made of my life for a while. It went from being my dream to being something I resented for a long while. I'd sacrificed everything to get to the top of the game. High school and college had been nonstop training and playing; one long hard fight to get to the top of the game. Friends and family had come second place to the game for as long as I could remember.

Even when my dad had been sick with cancer while I was in college, I'd focused more on the game. My family all said they understood, and kept on encouraging me, but looking back, I was a selfish little shit. They'd picked up my slack. Time with my family hadn't been the only casualty though, but no way was I letting my mind wander *there*. I'd spent a lot of time, and a ton of money in therapy, trying to squash the guilt I felt over the girl whose heart I broke when I left Savannah.

When I had been ruled unfit to play again, I hadn't wanted to come back here; there were so many reminders of the mistakes I had made. But with my parents not getting any younger, dad's previous bad health, and the opportunity to set up this place with my brother, I'd bitten the bullet and come home. Building a business with TJ has been much more fulfilling than anticipated. As much as it hurt to be here with the memories, it felt good to finally be able to be with my family.

I'm pulled from my musings when one of the gym instructors walks past wearing a wicked smile and not much else. Usually I'd be able to at least appreciate the view; not so much anymore, now I've seen Poppy again.

"Hey Score, how are ya?" She smirks as she passes.

That fucking nickname haunts me. I wouldn't hate it so much if I'd earned it on the field instead of off it. I was an idiot for a long time. It wasn't until I'd been on the edge of losing my career to my shitty lifestyle that I'd woken up and realized I was about to self-destruct. Dropping back down into my chair, I answer the ringing phone, hoping that whoever it is will give me at least a few minutes away from my own thoughts. A few minutes to try and push it all back into the box and lock it up. I've successfully managed to hide my feelings in for a long time now.

Once I hang up the phone, I try to keep my head on work. I don't know why I even bothered to come in today, I can't concentrate for shit. Throwing down the pen I've been doodling with, I stalk out of my office, letting the door slam shut behind me. Making my way up to the main floor, I weave through the equipment, giving head nods and brief smiles to the people I pass. Finding a treadmill in the corner that has no one around it, I pop in my earbuds and turn up some music that will hopefully drown out some of the excess noise in my head.

It's not long before I catch movement out of the corner of my eye. TJ steps onto the machine next to me and starts to run. I know he's waiting for me to tell him what the fuck is wrong with me. Slowing down my pace, I grab the t-shirt that's tucked in the back of my shorts and use it to wipe the sweat off my face.

"You ready to give it up, baby brother?" he asks as he steps off his own treadmill and moves to stand next to me. He's all of six minutes older than me, but he lives to make sure I remember it. Despite being twins, we're nothing alike. Running my hands over my head, I pull on my hair in frustration. I know it's pointless trying to hide it, so I just blurt it out.

"I saw Poppy last night."

The drink of water he just took sprays everywhere, covering me.

"What the fuck!" he shouts, staring at me, with eyes bugging out of his head. "Are you ok?"

And there it is. Why he's the best brother I could ever ask for. As much as he acts the idiot sometimes, he's always had my back.

"I don't know." I sigh. "Honestly? I don't know which way is up today," I say, letting myself drop down onto a nearby bench.

“What happened?”

“I had that kids charity thing last night, right?” I carry on when he nods. “I got there a few minutes after they’d seated everyone. She was at the table I was supposed to sit at. Right fucking next to me, man.”

I still can't believe it, and the shock is evident in my voice. TJ stares at me a beat, obviously waiting for me to say more, but I have nothing to say.

When I stay silent, he finally speaks. “So, what's the plan?”

“Huh?” His question takes me aback. “Plan for what?”

“How are you going to get her back?”

Isn’t that the million-dollar question?

Four

Poppy

Present

Finally wrestling the last dismantled cardboard box into the trash can, I slam the lid down and let out a, "Whoop!"

Since I'm alone in my secluded backyard, I shimmy my way up to my back deck and do a victory dance for Frank. "It might have taken me months, but that box in the trash means we are officially moved in!"

My dog just rolls his eyes and huffs at me. I guess he's not buying my fake cheer. In the seven days since I saw Keir, I've tried my best to pretend it just didn't happen. After picking up my clutch and mumbling incoherent apologies, I'd run as fast as my heels would allow, out of that room. There was sick part of me that hoped Keir would follow, chase me down and try and talk to me.

Elliott found me outside, choking back tears. Once she'd hustled us into a cab, I'd asked her not to talk about it. My head was too much of a jumble. How do I even process that? Seeing the guy that broke my heart, the one I thought I'd spend my life with? Make a family with? Ten years later, and he looked every bit as handsome as he always had. Once the cab had dropped me off at home and I'd said goodbye, I'd let the tears fall. I let myself feel for a few hours before I'd tamped down the emotions once again.

Grabbing the dog's big squishy face between my hands, I plant a loud kiss on his nose and give him a small shake. "Stop being a grump." He ignores me, instead rolling to his back for a belly rub. I indulge him for a few minutes until I hear my cell phone ringing in the kitchen.

Giving Frank one last scratch, I make my way inside the house through the open French doors. Pretty much the whole of the back wall of my tiny new home is glass and opens onto the sweetest little yard. As soon as I saw the kitchen and how it opened to the outdoors, I knew this was *the* house. The deck spans the length of the property, and just beyond that is a small lawn surrounded by trees and bushes. It's a little oasis within the hustle and bustle of Savannah.

There has always been something magical about this city for me. I'd never really had grand plans to spread my wings after college; being here felt right. When Keir and I had gotten serious, I'd resigned myself to moving away; for a while at least. But back then, I was in love and would have done anything to make us work.

Until the whole "broken heart and crushed dream" thing, obviously.

Rushing inside the house, I finally find my phone in between the pages of the book I was reading last night, and I see that it's Elliott calling. I've been avoiding her since that awful night last week. I answer the call, ready to turn on the fake cheer, but before I can get a word out, she shouts, "Maggie's, eight p.m. tonight. You and me, several bottles of wine, no arguments."

This is typical Elliott. I met my best friend the first day of college, when we were placed in the same dorm. We'd bonded over romance novels and ice cream. Despite me eventually leaving to go to New York, and her staying here in Georgia to get married and have kids, we've stayed very close, and she was a huge factor in my decision to move back here.

That choice had been a lot to take in. I hadn't been prepared for the gauntlet of emotions I'd had to run. Just being in the same city that held so many memories, both good and bad, had really messed with my head, and I couldn't face it. Having Elliott here to hold my hand through it has been a lifesaver. I know I'm being unfair to her by blocking her out like I have, but this is my coping mechanism—running away when things get hard.

"Hello to you too," I try to stall her. I know she wants to know where my head is.

"Poppy. I'm not playing anymore. You need to talk to me."

Well shit. She's giving me the "mom voice." I drop down onto a stool at the kitchen island in my new home, my new safe place, and take a fortifying breath.

"I can't go there again, El. You saw me...back then…I barely made it out," I stammer. My eyes are filling with tears and emotion clogs my throat. "It took me years to find *me* again, El. I need to keep moving forward."

I hear her sniffle through the phone and it makes my tears even more determined to fall.

"I'm scared, Pop. I just got you back here and I'm not ready for you to run again," she says in a voice that surprises me with how much emotion it holds.

Am I going to run again? I can't deny the temptation is strong. I could easily pack up and be gone in a few days. But I moved back here for a reason. I let my feelings over Keir, and what went on all that time ago, rule my life for far too long. I don't want to run. I don't want to be weak anymore. I don't want to be the woman that lets one man's actions dictate her whole life. I just want some peace.

"Elliott, I'm ok. Seeing him? Yeah, it shocked me. But I'm going to be ok. I'm not running. I promise," I say, really meaning it, I have no plans to run this time. Not yet anyway.

Hearing her gulp, I wait for her to get herself together.

"Ok, I'm here, though. Whenever you need me."

I'm so thankful she's letting this drop; for now, at least. Feeling like the best thing to do is to rip off the proverbial band-aid off, I push down my anxiety and ask, "Anyway, did I hear someone mention wine?"

"I can't *not* look." Elliott laughs, bent over the high table where we're seated. We got here earlier to find that it was speed dating night. We've been giggling our asses off at how horribly awkward some of the dates have been. Some of the couples have been terribly mismatched. We're well into our second bottle of wine and I'm so glad I came. I needed to get out of my own head for a while. Wiping away the tears of mirth that have filled my eyes most of the night, I sigh.

"Thank you." I swallow the lump of unexpected emotion that clogs my throat. "I needed this, *you*. Thank you for being the best, best friend a girl could need."

El gives me a watery smile as she squeezes my hand that's resting on the table top.

"Love you too, girl. I'm always here. Well, not here exactly, because Pete would lose his mind if I left him with the kids too often, but you know what I mean," she jokes.

"Ok, that's enough of the sappy stuff. Let's finish these and go for food. I'm starving, and I'm in need of carbs to soak up some of this booze."

Waiting for Elliott to use the restroom before we leave, I wander closer to the door. I'm not paying attention to where I'm going and I walk straight into someone coming my way with a tray of drinks in their hand. The tray flies up and gets crushed between our bodies before it falls to the floor. The full bottles flip with it, soaking the guy's shirt before smashing to the ground at our feet. A hand reaches out to grab my arm to stop me from doing the same. Looking up, I see the guy I just trampled is not much taller than me, with long greasy hair and a sharp face. He's wearing a deep scowl.

"Shit! I'm so sorry…" My voice trails off as the hand tightens on me, making me wince in pain.

"Watch where you're going in the future," he snarls at me, as his eyes flick up and down my body and his lips spread into an arrogant smirk. His yellow teeth and strong beer breath make my stomach revolt. "I suggest you get your pretty little ass up to that counter and buy me new beers." His voice is a menacing growl that has me shrinking in fear. I'm not sure I've had someone look at me with such bitterness before.

"Of course," I whisper, fear clogging my throat. "I really am sorry."

"Unless you want to repay me some other way..."

Before he can say anything more, the guy disappears from in front of me. I don't have time to work out what's going on before I'm turned around and a handsome face dips down to look at me.

"Are you ok?"

"TJ?" I say, before I promptly burst into tears. I'm a little drunk, a lot overwhelmed, and completely shocked that the man rescuing me is one I haven't seen in years.

"Hey now, it's ok." He pulls me in for a hug and pats me on the back.

"Thank you for saving me, that guy was a dick." I do an ugly laugh-cry thing, trying to lighten the mood and failing miserably.

"Don't thank me, he's the one that saw it happen." He nods over my shoulder, and I don't need to turn to see who's standing there. For the second time in a few weeks, my past has turned up at just the right time to save me.

Taking in a fortifying breath, I squeeze TJ's hands that have been holding mine. He gives me a nod; I assume he's trying to silently communicate that I'll be ok. Wiping away the last of my tears, I slowly turn, seeing Keir walking in through the door, just a few feet away. He's in faded jeans and a white tee that looks rumpled, a small tear at the collar. I swear the worn leather jacket he has on is the same one I bought him for our one and only Christmas together.

He's got his hands stuffed into his front pockets and his face is giving nothing away. God, he's even more beautiful than he was before. He's huge now, all broad shoulders and intimidating height. He's still looks like *my* Keir though. Last week, I'd not gotten a chance to appreciate all that he now was. I'd been too quick to run away.

"Thank you." My words are tiny, lost within the loud noise of the still bustling bar. I know he's heard me though because he swallows hard before he takes two steps closer to me.

"No problem, Lolly-pop. He won't be bothering you again."

I'm glad I'm somewhat numbed by alcohol and adrenaline, otherwise I'm sure that nickname would be enough to drop me to my knees. Keir had started using it the very first night we met. Neither of us say anything else, we just keep staring. The silent exchange is broken when Elliott comes barreling into me.

"Oh my God! Are you ok? What the hell happened?" She dumps her bag on the nearest table and pulls me into a hug.

"I'm fine. These two were here to save me." I motion to where Keir and his brother stand, just off to the side of us, having a quiet conversation of their own.

"So much for me sneaking us out before you saw them." She laughs before turning to thank the guys for helping me.

"You knew they were here?" I'm shocked she didn't say anything; she's usually terrible at keeping secrets.

"I saw them when they came in. I didn't want you to freak out."

She's not even a little sorry.

Now that the excitement of the last few minutes have worn off, I'm itching to get away from the awkwardness I'm feeling.

"Well, thanks again, but we'd better get going."

"Can I give you guys a ride anywhere?" TJ asks, and just as I'm about decline, Elliott claps and does a little jump.

"That's perfect!" She links her arm through his and heads to the doors, making plans as if it hasn't been years since she's seen him.

"Are you sure you're ok?"

Turning my head, I see Keir has moved even closer, and I have to tip my head back to see him clearly. I used to love his height; the way he would tower over me, my head barely passing his shoulder. He always made me feel so safe when he was around. It's crazy, but I still feel the urge to bury my face in his chest and wrap my arms around his waist. My body doesn't seem to care that we haven't been together in forever.

Tucking my hair back behind my ear, I smile a little and nod. "Yep, I'm fine. I promise."

I give him the fakest smile I've ever given. He'd have to be dense not to realize I'm bold-faced lying.

"I was wondering if we could…" He starts to speak, and it's almost adorable how unsure of himself he looks but, hell no, I am *not* doing this with him. I'm not ready to get into a conversation with him. Hell, even being in the same room as him is torture. I obviously won't be able to avoid running into him, but that doesn’t mean I have to like it.

“Let’s not do this, Keir,” I say, stopping him from finishing what he was about to say.

I need to get out of here fast, so I make a move toward the door. The quicker I can get away from him, the better. I hear him let out a sigh from behind, before he moves to hold the door open for me. I don't look at him as I pass, but I notice he doesn’t leave me much room in the doorway, and I have to turn to the side to avoid touching him.

A few minutes later, I find myself seated in the back of a huge truck, Elliott next to me, chatting away, ignoring the fact I’m obviously pissed at her. TJ sits in the front passenger seat, half-twisted to face us in the back, so that he can talk to El, and Keir is driving.

I continue to sulk, refusing to join in with their conversation. Why am I here? I should have refused. Keir looks mad, and I don't know if it’s because I refused to speak to him or if it’s because I’m here, period. He’s gripping the steering wheel so tightly, I’m surprised it hasn’t snapped off. Like me, he’s not said a word.

As we pull up outside of Elliott's house, I move to take my seatbelt off.

“What are you doing?” she asks me, looking confused.

“Getting out? I’ll get a cab from here.” When I say it, I swear I see Keir’s shoulders relax, as if he’s relieved.

"Get back in here, Poppy, we'll get you home." It's TJ that speaks; Keir keeps his head pointedly staring elsewhere.

"Just send me a text when you get home. Thanks, guys!"

El jumps out of the truck and slams the door before I can argue with her.

And so begins the single most awkward car journey I've ever been on. I'm totally going to kick her ass the next time I see her

Five

Keir

Present

I'm going to murder my brother. I'm going to make sure it's a long and painful death too.

It's torture listening to him make small talk with Poppy while I feel like my world has been tipped on its head. I'm still filled with rage at seeing that creep with his hands on her. It had taken everything in me not to beat the shit out of him after I dragged him outside. I think he understood my warning loud and clear after I threw his ass out of there.

I've had a week to try and work out how I feel about seeing Poppy again. A week to try and make some sense of the mess of emotions seeing her brought up. And I *still* have no clue how I'm feeling. Listening to TJ try and get her to speak is painful. She obviously doesn't want to be here, and I can't say I blame her. I'm guessing she still hates me.

It only takes about ten minutes to get to her house and I'm not at all surprised to see she lives so close to Elliott. They were always close. I'm glad she still has her.

I park the truck in the space Poppy points out to me, and she has the door open before I've even stopped.

"Thanks guys, goodnight!" she shouts, with that horrible fake smile on her face again. It might be irrational, but every time I see it, I want to punch something.

"You're not going to just let her go, are you?" TJ looks at me incredulously when I don't follow her immediately.

"Did you not see how uncomfortable she was? Why would I make it worse by following her?" I scoff.

"You are an idiot."

He turns to open his door but before he even has his belt off, I'm out my door. My long legs quickly catch up to Poppy as she reaches her front door, keys in hand. I have no idea what the fuck I'm doing, but I'm sick of watching her walk away from me.

"Hey." My voice startles her, and she jumps, her hand coming to her throat in shock.

"Keir! Dammit, you shouldn't do that!" She reaches out and slaps my shoulder as she gives a nervous laugh and, for a split second, it's like we've never been apart. As if the past ten years don't stand between us like a brick wall.

The moment is lost when she blinks and looks away. Clearing her throat, she looks back up at me nervously, and my arms burn with the need to reach out and touch her. I can't tell what she's thinking. She looks terrified, but beneath that, I think she's feeling just as confused as I am.

Confusion is good; it isn't hate. Confusion means there is a chance for me, that some of the good feelings are still in there somewhere. Her confusion means I've made up my mind. I want her back and I'm not stopping until I get her.

"I was wondering if you're free this week sometime? Maybe we could grab a coffee? Dinner, maybe?"

As soon as the words are out of my mouth, I know it was the wrong thing to say; I pushed too hard too fast. Her shoulders slump, and she looks at me sadly.

"I'm not sure that's a good idea." I notice she doesn't say no, so I try and press my luck.

"Come on. Just two old friends catching up."

"Really?" The incredulous look she gives me makes me smile. "Old friends?" she asks, with a head tilt.

"Yeah, old friends. I'd like to catch up, find out what you've been up to since I saw you last."

"Again, I don't think that's a good idea."

"I do."

"Keir!" She laughs again, but I just keep looking at her, not saying anything. I can see the wheels turning in her mind.

"Seriously?" Her voice is soft when she asks.

She looks at me pleadingly, and I don't know if she wants me to keep pushing her, or to leave her alone. Now that she's back, I know I won't be able to leave her alone. Not until I'm certain she doesn't want me.

"Come on, just a few hours," I coax, giving her the smile that usually gets me anything I want. I just pray it works this time too.

The look on her pretty face stays indiscernible while she thinks of what to say. Even though there's not much light out here, she still looks beautiful. Her hair, lighter than I'm used to it being, is down around her shoulders, and I can't help but reach out and touch it. It's that movement that snaps her out of her own head.

On a deep sigh, she says, "I'm going to be honest with you. I'm only just getting settled back in here and so far, it's been hard. Much harder than I thought. I…I need some time." She smiles sadly at me. Looking at her standing in front of me, her arms wrapped around herself defensively, makes me want to kick my own ass. "I'm not ready to deal with the feelings seeing you brings back."

I want her back, but I'm not going to be a jerk about it. She's asking for time, and I can give her that. For now, at least.

"Ok, Lolly-pop." Her eyes flare at the use of her nickname. "I can give you that. For now," I say with a smirk, causing her to shake her head at me.

"Good night, Keir. Thank you again, for the ride home *and* for saving me earlier."

Giving me a smile, she turns to wave to TJ before she goes inside. Not wanting to leave her, now that I've found her again, I stay on her porch for a minute, until I hear the lock slide into place and see a light come on inside.

Six

Poppy

Past

Wiping my hair back off my sweaty face, I heave my bag off the airport carousel in front of me.

This is my first time flying alone, and I'm starting to regret my plan to surprise Keir. I could use his help with this stupid luggage. Once I finally work out where I'm going, I jump into a cab and give the driver the address for Keir's apartment building.

It's been seven months since he left for Seattle and two months since I saw him last. This separation has been so much harder than I ever thought it would be. Between school, working two jobs, and Keir's insane schedule with the team, we can't seem to find time to be together. The phone calls and Skype sessions that started as a daily thing have become few and far between. The promised trips to see each other have been cancelled, usually due to commitments with the team. I have a feeling that Keir has struggled to find his place here, and bonding with the other guys has been a priority. I get it, but I just wish it wasn't at my expense.

The last two weeks have been the worst. We've not spoken for three days now. After missing *another* call because I'd picked up a second shift at the coffee shop, Keir had left me a message, basically accusing me of punishing him with my silence. Was I doing that?

After he cancelled yet another trip back to Savannah to see me, I hadn't wanted to pretend I was ok. I was hurt and angry. Not necessarily at Keir, just at the whole situation. Instead of fighting it out over the phone, again, I'd opted to take a breather. A day to calm down so that I wouldn't say something I might regret. We have another year of this, and if we can't sort out our communication problems, there is no way we will survive it.

That's why I'm here. I need to make as much effort as I expect from Keir.

After crying to my brother about how down I've been feeling, he surprised me with an airplane ticket to fly out here and a week off from work. I don't know what he used to bribe my boss to get it, but I'm not going to complain.

Leaning my head against the cab window, I take in the dreary Seattle scenery flying past me. I hate this city. I hate how everything is gray and damp feeling. I hate that I'll be moving here soon. I'll be here, in a city I don't know, with no friends and no Keir most of the time. The downside to falling in love with a professional athlete, the part no one tells you about, is how bone-crushingly lonely it can be. The year we were together while he played in college was hard, but at least there I had my friends to get me through it. How am I going to survive it here?

Before my maudlin thoughts can get out of control, I notice we're turning into the apartment complex Keir shares with one of the other new guys on the team. We're supposed to be looking for somewhere for us to live together next year, but that's another thing that gets pushed to the back burner every time I ask about it. For now, it suits him to live with someone else. I've met Kyle, his roommate, once before, and he seems like a good guy.

The driver pulls up in front of the doors and once I've paid him, he lifts my bags out for me. I'm about to walk into the building when I see Kyle blow past in the flashy Range Rover he drives. I wave, but he doesn't notice me. I hope Keir hasn't left yet. I didn't plan this trip very well, and I'm praying I haven't made a mistake by coming here.

Stepping inside the lobby, I look around for the doorman that's supposed to be there to announce any visitors. I wait a minute, but he doesn't return, so I make my way over to the elevator. As I'm waiting for the doors to open, a woman walks quickly into the lobby. She's pretty, with long blonde bed hair that's wild and flowing down her back, and she's wearing a short dress, her heels in her hands. My guess is she's doing the walk of shame, or stride of pride, as Elliott would call it.

When we both step into the elevator and I press the button for the top floor. I notice she doesn't select one of her own. We ride up in a silence that doesn't feel comfortable. I'm not sure if it's nerves over how Keir is going to react to my surprise, or something else.

The doors slide open on a quiet *ding,* and I step out ahead of the woman. Taking a deep breath to steady my nerves, I knock on the door before I can chicken out. It's not until I hear the lock slide back in the door that I notice the blonde from the elevator is standing behind me.

I don't look at her as the door swings open.

I don't look at her as Keir's tired face fills my vision, looking heartachingly beautiful.

I don't look at her as his pain-filled eyes sweep over me, only to keep going before stopping on her.

I don't look at her as his face falls, and something that looks a lot like guilt washes over his features.

"What are you doing here?" His rough voice startles me, and I don't immediately realize it's me he's speaking to, but it is.

Why is he asking me that and not her?

Why hasn't he asked her who she is?

Why do I get the feeling my world has just been irrevocably shaken?

When I don't say anything, he looks over my head again and speaks to her for the first time.

"Sorry sweetheart, now's not a good time. I got your number, though. I'll call you later."

Her eyes flick to me nervously before she speaks. “Um, actually, I…uh...I just realized I left my phone here. Can I get it quickly? Then I…uh…I’ll let you two…get back to…uh…whatever this is.”

When she moves to go into the apartment, I realize I’m still out in the hall.

I just flew hours to surprise my boyfriend, and I’m standing in the hall, not saying a word, while he makes a date with someone that obviously just rolled out of his bed.

White-hot anger blazes through me.

“What the fuck is going on?” I grind out through teeth that are clamped together so tight, it’s a miracle they don't shatter. He stares at me a beat, legs planted wide, and the strong, safe arms I love so much crossed on his bare chest.

“You tell me what’s going on, sweetheart,” he says in a mocking voice that make me want to punch him in his throat. “I thought this is what we were doing now? I assumed, since you were having guys stay at your apartment, I could do the same.”

I have no clue what he’s talking about, and his condescending tone is about to push me over the edge.

“Don't play fucking games with me, Keir. If you couldn’t survive a few weeks without getting your dick wet, you should have just told me.”

He has the nerve to smirk at me. Who the fuck is this guy? And what the hell has he done with the sweet man I fell in love with?

"Why are you even here, Poppy? Your new man tired of you already?"

Is this a joke? Confusion clouds my mind, mixing with the anger that's slowly building inside me.

"I have no idea what you are talking about!" I shout.

His face hardens in anger and he leans forward, getting into my face. He stops when his eyes are level with mine. The chocolate pools are a hurricane of anger and hurt.

"Save it. I saw the picture. Do you realize how many people sent me that? How many of our so-called friends couldn't wait to send me the picture of you, looking very fucking cozy, cuddled up to some guy on your doorstep two days ago."

I wrack my brain, trying to think what the hell he could be talking about, when it suddenly hits me. My blood thrums through me as anger over takes my entire body. Throwing my backpack onto the floor, I dig around until I find my phone. Scrolling through until I find what I'm looking for, I push the phone in his face, but he stubbornly refuses to look.

"This guy, Keir?" I scoff, my voice never wavering. It's steady and strong. I won't let him see that he's just decimated me. I can see from the look on his face that he's confused by my reaction. His eyes flick down to the phone and he flinches at the picture on the screen. The one I forced Duke to take before he left my apartment after his surprise visit a few days ago. Someone must have saw us saying goodbye. I can imagine how quickly they would have made sure Keir saw it too.

"If you'd bothered to answer your fucking phone once in a while, you would know that my brother visited me this week."

His eyes flash to mine but he doesn't say a word. His jaw moves, as if he's trying to find words, but there's nothing there. His body is frozen in place.

"That's right. He knew I was struggling without you, so he surprised me with a flight out here."

Taking one last look at the man I had all my hopes and dreams pinned on, all I feel is disgust and anger. He doesn't deserve my explanations, not anymore. I want to shout and scream at him. Hit and kick him. But the need to get the fuck out of here as quickly as I can wins, before he sees what he's done to me, how he's ripped my heart clean out of my chest and shredded it.

"Goodbye, Keir," I choke out before turning and running back toward the elevator, realizing at the last minute that if I stand there and wait for the doors to open, Keir and *that girl* are going to hear the sob that's about to explode from within me. I manage to push through the door before I feel a large hand grab me and spin me around.

"Lolly-pop, stop. I'm sorry. I'm so fucking sorry. Let me explain." His voice is cracking with emotion, causing my tears to bubble up even further. Anger and instinct overtake me and, before I can stop myself, my fist flies out and connects with his face.

Both of us freeze, chests heaving. I have to get out of here. The walls are closing in on me, and I can't fucking deal with this. I don't know who I am right now.

"Just come inside and talk to me. Please. This whole thing is fucked up."

"No!" My voice is scathing. "What's fucked up is you. I *never* want to see you again."

The next words to leave my mouth are the three words I never thought I'd say to this man.

"I hate you."

I don't know what he sees on my face when I say it, but it's enough for him to let me go this time. I throw myself down the steps as fast as I can, desperate to be away from this whole situation.

Seven

Poppy

Me: this is me not talking to you btw

El: You're doing a great job of it so far.

Me: I'm serious. You're no longer my BFF.

El: *bored face*

El: You'll thank me when you finally get some decent D back in your life

Me: BYE.

I throw my cell phone back into my workout bag. Elliott has been dodging my calls since she abandoned me last night. I tossed and turned all night, thoughts of Keir keeping me awake. I finally managed to get a few hours, just before dawn, only to be plagued by dreams of that horrible day.

I barely remembered leaving the apartment block after I told him I hated him. After stumbling down the stairs and making it to a nearby coffee shop, I'd called my brother. He wanted to fly out and beat the crap out of Keir. By the time he'd calmed down, and I'd stopped sobbing, he'd managed to get me on a flight back to Savannah the same day.

The weeks after that were some of the hardest I ever lived through. I'd been broken. I couldn't help feeling like it was my fault. Keir was always a good guy. I, never in million years, could have imagined him cheating on me. We'd had ups and downs, silly arguments and such, but never anything like this. I knew being apart was taking its toll on us, but I didn't even recognize the man that opened the apartment door that day.

That first month, I'd been a shell of the person I was before. I didn't eat, and I barely slept. Elliott and my brother had needed to step in and stop me from spiraling even further out of control. Gradually, with their help, I'd worked my way through it and the me that came out the other side was different. Harder. Seeing him again is bringing a lot of bad feelings to the surface and I'm just not ready to face them.

Stepping through the doors of the gym, I realize just how nice this place actually is. Flex Health and Fitness is a new addition to Savannah and from what I've heard, it's super fancy. The reception area is large, bright, and airy. A sleek white desk with modern computer screens lines the wall to the right. There's a beautiful brunette woman seated behind the desk, with the phone to her ear. She's talking quietly and I don't want to interrupt her, so I move to look at the displays of fitness equipment dotted around the space. The displays of protein shakes and bars are all perfectly arranged. Everything is lined up, with nothing out of place.

I hadn't planned to join a gym, but my bid had been the winning one at the auction last month, so I bit the bullet and decided to come in and sign up. Considering I'm new to the whole fitness thing, I'm feeling extremely out of place. Once the receptionist is finished with her call and I've explained why I'm here, she offers to take me on a tour of the facilities.

As we make our way around the place, I learn her name is Lucy and she not only covers the new signups, she also teaches some fitness classes. The majority of the equipment looks like torture devices to me, so I have a feeling I'll be spending most of my time here with her.

The gym itself is huge. Row after row of exercise bikes and other things I can't name fill the cavernous space. Everything is gleaming and looks brand new. The thing that stands out for me is that the people here seem to be serious about it. There are no posers flexing in the huge mirrored walls. No gym bunnies in overly skimpy outfits. Lucy shows me the pool and changing facilities, the studios where she holds her classes, and finally, a big set of doors that are unmarked.

"That's the basement. It's open to members, but that's where the boxing rings and other equipment are. I don't think you'll need to go down there much, but I can show you around if you want?"

"Yeah, I don't think that's necessary," I say, causing us both to laugh. We make our way back to the front desk, and I'm feeling much less intimidated than I did an hour ago.

"And that's pretty much everything. I'll get you a list of classes, and you can sign up for them online if you'd prefer."

"That's perfect, thanks for your help. I was scared out of my mind before I came in here."

"Yeah, you didn't do a great job at hiding it." She says it a way that doesn't embarrass me; she's a natural at making people feel at ease, and I can easily see why she was employed here. Once I've signed everything I need and collected my membership, I start to make my way outside.

As I push through the glass doors, I collide with a body on its way in. Letting out a loud gasp, I watch as my bag hits the floor and my phone skitters out, landing a few feet away. The open bottle in my hands crumples, water flying up and soaking us both.

"Poppy, are you ok?" I don't need to look up to know the hands holding onto me belong to Keir.

"Seriously? I don't see you for ten years, and suddenly you're everywhere I go?"

I can't help but sound snarky; the frustration I'm feeling is just too much. Anger heats me from the inside out. How dare he keep doing this to me? I just want some peace from the emotions running rampant through me lately.

His arms don't loosen their grip on me, but I do see him fight a smile. Stepping back out of his grasp, I notice what he's wearing. Black, skintight compression pants, with loose, but oh-so-short running shorts over the top. His now soaked white Under Armor tee is like a second skin, it's so tight.

Damn, he looks good.

He reaches up, peeling the wet t-shirt from his body. I try so hard not to look, I really do, but that body was not made to be ignored.

Keir clears his throat and it takes me a second to realize I've been staring too long at his chest. Flicking my eyes up to his, I see he's given up fighting the smile and it's now an annoying smirk on his face.

"It's nice to see you too," he says, as his eyes trace my body the way mine just did his. I notice a flare of desire is evident when they hit my chest.

"Good morning, boss." Lucy pops up next to me, passing me my phone. "Poppy is our newest member. She was the winner of the charity auction thing you donated to."

She smiles widely, looking between Keir and I as we continue to stare at one another, and I have to fight the groan of frustration that threatens to leave me. *Of course* he just so happens to own the gym I've just joined, why wouldn't he?

"Poppy and I go way back," he tells Lucy, the smirk now a full-blown grin. Before she can answer that, I, once again, turn to leave.

“Thanks again, see you soon!” I plaster on the fake cheer that is a necessity these days, turn for the door, and get the hell out of there.

I’m almost to my car when I hear my name being called from behind me.

“Poppy! Can I talk to you real quick?” Keir asks, as he makes his way toward me, both fists clenched at his side again. Is he doing that to stop himself from touching me, like he did when he touched my hair last night? God, I want him to touch me almost as badly as I *don't* want him to.

It's amazing how all the years apart have done nothing to dampen my attraction to this man. That scares the shit out of me. He broke my heart, and I still just want him to wrap those amazing arms around me. For him to pick me up like he used to, before kissing me so thoroughly, my toes would curl in my shoes. I should hate him. I’m a mass of conflicted feelings and that’s what has me pissed.

“What can I do for you?” I purposely keep the tone of my voice flat, trying to act like being around him bores me. I notice that his brows pull down in a frown when I speak.

“I was just wondering if you’d thought about what I said last night?”

Is this man serious? Did I think about it? No, I didn't think about it… I *obsessed* over it. I ran the few sentences we exchanged through my head back and forth until dawn this morning.

He mistakes my silence for confusion, so he tries to clarify what he meant. “About us going out sometime?”

“It’s not going to happen, Keir. Please, let this drop?”

I don’t know why it comes out as a question. Keeping my voice firm is a nightmare. The part of me that wants him back in my life fights hard to be heard, but I’m not going there again. I’m not putting my heart on the line, just to have him stomp all over it when things inevitably go wrong.

He doesn’t say anything more, and I don’t look at him before turning once again to get in my car and start it up. I pull out of the parking lot and, looking in my rearview mirror, I see him watching me leave. He doesn’t follow. Just like he didn't follow me the last time I left.

Keir

Past

Parking my truck in my usual space outside the apartment, I can't bring myself to leave the quiet of the cab just yet. I take a minute to lean my head back, close my eyes, and listen to the rain beat down on the roof. The staccato rhythm almost lulls me to sleep.

The last month without Poppy has taken its toll on me, body and mind. Sleep is a long-forgotten luxury these days and every time I close my eyes, I see her face. See it twisted in pain, then quickly turning to anger. That moment when realization took over and the joy leaked from her features. The same moment my stomach took root somewhere around my ankles and hasn't come back up since.

As if that wasn't bad enough, training has been kicking my ass. Lack of concentration and being pummeled by three-hundred-pound guys is not a combination I'd recommend to anyone. I need to get over this. I made a decision not to go after her, beg for her to listen to me, or let me try and explain.

This life isn't for her. Who I am now isn't right for her. She deserves the world. She put her faith in me, in us, and I let her down. I knew her insecurities, how she was struggling with being so far apart, and at the first bump in the road, I messed up. Monumentally. I need to learn to move on without her, even if it kills me.

My cell starts blasting out the obnoxious ringtone my brother set for himself. Looking at the screen, I internally debate whether or not to answer. I've been avoiding my family since I told them that Poppy wasn't a part of my life anymore. I can't handle another round of him telling me what an idiot I am.

Declining the call, I push open the door. I don't make any effort to try and rush through the rain, instead letting it soak me; I can't get up the energy to care right now. Grabbing my gym bag from the back of the truck, I make my way upstairs. Throwing a quick wave toward Mike, the concierge, I say a quiet "thank fuck" that he's stuck on a call and not trying to get me into another football conversation.

Now all I need is for Kyle to be out, so I don't have to listen to him dig into me over how miserable I am. His incessant crap talk about how I need to get out and fuck someone to get over Poppy is driving me crazy. The idea of going out there and having fun guts me. The thought of touching someone else makes me feel physically sick, which is the biggest fucking irony, considering how I ended up in this situation.

Stepping into the elevator, I turn to face the doors; looking in the mirror is the last thing I need right now. I don't need a reminder of shitty I look. How my hair needs to be cut, how dark the circles are under my eyes are, or how I'm losing weight because eating and going to the gym, like I should be, are just beyond my capabilities right now.

When the doors slide open and I make my way down the hall, I'm stopped in my tracks when I see who is sitting on the floor outside the apartment door.

Poppy.

Her head is back against the hard wood of the door, her legs stretched out in front of her, crossed at the ankles. She's bundled up against the cool air outside with a long scarf wrapped around her beautiful neck. She's sleeping, but it's still easy to see how gorgeous she is. Her long dark hair is loose around her face, long eyelashes resting on her slightly pink cheeks, those soft lips parted the tiniest amount.

Even asleep and looking as stunning as ever, I can see how tired she looks. Her face isn't relaxed, like it normally would be. I can see faint smudges under her eyes. I notice her coat and hair are dry, so she must have been here some time already because it's been raining all day. Dropping down onto my knees next to her, I can't resist the urge to touch her. I gently run the tips of my fingers from the top of her face down to her chin, reveling in the fact that she turns into my touch, nuzzling into the palm of my hand. Why did I have to fuck this up so bad? The fissure in my cracked heart widens even more when she whispers a breathy "Keir" in her sleep.

Sliding my hand from her chin around to cup the back of her head, I gently wake her up.

"Poppy. Wake up, baby girl, you'll be sore sleeping down here."

As her eyes flicker open, there's the briefest of seconds where she looks at me like she used to, with love and so much affection, but it's gone by the time she blinks her eyes. I know that later I'll question whether or not it was ever really there. She twists her head to the side, so I have no choice but to drop my hand from her hair, and she moves to stand in front of me. She won't even look me in the eyes. When she speaks, her words are so full of pain they almost drop me to me back to my knees.

"I need to know what I did wrong. It couldn't have just been because you saw a picture. You and I were bigger than assumptions." The first tear slides down her face and drops off her chin. "I can't move on until I know what I did wrong."

I know I can't keep this up, I need to tell her the truth. Rushing forward, I try to pull her to me, but she quickly raises her hands in front of her, as a sort of warning to back off. Even though it kills me to do it, I take a step back, giving her the space she needs.

"Baby girl, at the end of the day, it wasn't you. Never you, I promise." I can feel my throat close up as a ball of emotion lodges itself there. "If you don't ever believe another word I say, please at least believe that."

My voice cracks. I'm begging her to believe me, but my words only seem to make her cry even harder and

I'm not able to stand and watch her anymore. I have her in my arms in a heartbeat, and she's soon gripping the back of my shirt while she cries into my chest. My murmured apologies do nothing to ease her distress.

Shifting her slightly to my side, I manage to get the door opened and us shuffled into the living room. Seeing her like this is killing me; my girl is usually so full of life, ready to rip my balls off and feed them to me whenever she feels wronged. This isn't the girl that left here a month ago. The one who slapped me and told me she hated me. The one that walked out with her head held high.

Managing to remove her coat and scarf, I get her seated on the sofa without a fight while I perch on the coffee table in front of her.

"Baby girl, let me go make you a drink." I don't miss her flinch at my endearment, but old habits die hard with her, and she'll always be that to me. No matter what comes from her being here today.

"Just tell me." Her tears are flowing again now, as she grips onto my forearm tightly, not letting me go. "I don't understand how we got here. You promised we would be ok, you said we would make it work. I know I made it hard for you, I know I was needy and probably acted like a brat, but you promised." Her last words came out on a cracked sob.

I did this to her, I broke this amazing woman down. Her words circle around and around in my mind. Why? Why didn't I just stop, why did I ever doubt her?

“I didn’t sleep with her.” The words fall out of my mouth before I can stop them.

Time seems to still; it’s as if all the air has been sucked from the room by the power of my words alone. She’s frozen on the seat in front of me, her eyebrows furrowed so deeply they almost meet in the middle.

“What?” she breathes out. My heart is raging in my chest, and I’m pretty sure she’s feeling the same right now. “What the fuck do you mean?”

She leans forward, her hands gripping mine that are now covering the shame on my face. “You told me… You said you… I saw you! And...and...*her*.”

She’s tripping over the words as her mind tries in vain to process what I’m saying. Fuck, she’s on the verge of hyperventilating. I put my hands on her shoulders and try to get her to focus on me.

“I’m sorry, Poppy. So, so sorry. I can explain, I promise, but you need to calm down. You need to breathe for me.”

When her eyes lock on mine, she takes a deep breath. I can't believe we’ve come to this. Knowing that I’ve destroyed her will haunt me forever, that I know for sure. The only thing for me to do now is tell her the truth.

“I know what I said and what you saw, but I didn’t actually have sex with her.” And I’m telling the truth. As fuzzy as my head had been that morning, I’d known that things hadn’t gone all the way. Too many whiskies meant I'd passed out before I could make an even bigger mistake.

Why hadn't I admitted this to Poppy right away? That was a hard question to answer, but as soon as I'd heard those words, "I hate you," I'd known I had to let her go. I was ruining her life. Weeks of letting her down and hearing disappointment in her voice had been taking its toll on me. I was sick of living under the weight of her expectations and instead of being a man and talking to her, I'd taken the coward's way out. I'd let her think I'd fucked someone else.

The fact that I hadn't managed to go through with it didn't make me any more of a good guy. It didn't negate her pain. I should have let her keep thinking it. I wasn't strong enough to make this work with her, I knew it was only a matter of time before we broke under the strain of the miles between us. Me putting football and the team over her, us, was an inevitability. One I wasn't man enough to stop.

Looking at her here, now, in front of me and, fuck, I see it in her eyes.

Hope.

She thinks we can fix this.

And seeing that makes me feel like an even bigger piece of shit. I need her to hate me. I need to give her the chance to find someone that will choose her.

Choose her over everything. Always.

Pushing her hands away slightly, I do what I think is the right thing.

"I would have, though." The words are stuck in my throat. "I would have done it, ok? I physically couldn't do it, but I tried. I fucking tried. Do you understand what I'm saying? I tried to cheat on you."

I see the effect the words have. Like tiny bullets piercing her, one after the other, her body reacts, like each one spoken is a barb scoring a direct hit.

"I wanted you to hurt like I hurt. I'm sorry. That's the only word I have, and I know it will never be enough, but that's it. If I could go back and stop myself, I would. If I could go back and listen to what my brain was telling me, I would, in a heartbeat."

I have no idea why or how it happens, but the next second, I find her in my arms. Her small hands cling to my bowed head that is somehow resting on her stomach as she stands between my seated thighs.

"I don't know how to say goodbye to you," she sobs, making my hands grip even tighter onto her. "My brain knows that this is it, but my heart just can't catch up."

I pull gently on her hips and as she falls to her knees on the floor in front to me, I slide down to meet her within a second. The magnitude of the pain in her eyes is astounding. I can't keep looking at her because the guilt is suffocating me. I know what she means; my brain and my heart aren't even reading the same book, let alone the same page through all this. But it's my conscience that wins. That part of me knows I have to let her go.

Deciding to twist the knife just that little bit more, I lean in and kiss her so gently on the side of her lips that

I'm not even sure she feels it. Shifting back, I look at the most beautiful face I've ever seen, the one I know will haunt me forever after today.

I couldn't say which of us was the first to lean back in, whose lips touched the other's first.

All I know is that within seconds, her taste floods my mouth.

Within minutes, we're both naked, undone.

Within hours, I wake up, and she's gone.

Nine

Keir

Present

"Letting her walk away again? Will you ever learn?"

Just what I need, my brother all over my business. Again.

"Why do you give a shit anyway?" I gripe at him. Hearing the disappointment that tinges his voice pisses me off.

"Because I miss her. We all miss her."

I don't want to hear this, it's too much to deal with. Turning away from him, I go to move back inside. My family members were all so fucking disappointed when Poppy and I didn't work out. My parents were so angry when I told them what had gone on, I wasn't sure my mom was going to forgive me. I'm stopped by his next words.

“You know something? We miss you too.” His voice softens. “You changed after she left. You’ve always been my brother, but you just weren’t the same.”

I keep my back to him, but I stop walking as he continues. “You did a decent job at hiding it, but the pain was always there, in the back of your eyes.”

“What can I do?” He steps up next to me and we make our way back to my office. “You saw her. She doesn’t want anything to do with me.”

Dropping down into my chair, I swing my legs up onto the desk and throw my head back against the leather seat.

“She turned you down once, and that’s it? That’s all the effort she’s worth?”

“Of course she’s worth more, but she asked me to leave her alone! What the fuck am I supposed to do with that?” My frustrated voice is loud in the quiet room.

“I know you still carry a lot of guilt about what went down, but you have to stop kicking your own ass for it.”

Can I do that? I wish it was that simple. As much as I want to chase her down and make her listen to me, if she doesn’t want that, who am I to ignore her?

“I saw you and her.”

I look at him, confused. I have no idea what he’s talking about. “When?”

"Last night, when you went to walk her to her door. The way she was looking at you, man, the way you were looking at each other?" he says with a shake of his head. "If there is any chance you can work this out, you need to try with everything you have."

"She told me to leave her alone, I can't ignore that."

"Can you ignore the fact that the only person you ever loved just fell back into your lap?" When I stay silent, he keeps on. "You made a mistake. Back then, you should have held on tighter."

"*She* left *me*! *She* snuck out in the middle of the night. *She* didn't give me a choice," I cut in, but he ignores me and carries on.

"You should have held on tighter. She needed you to prove to her she was worth chasing. That you chose her, that you were sorry, and that what you had was worth fighting for."

"Are you done?" I can't keep hearing this stuff. I know I fucked everything up, and having it rubbed in my face is not helping.

"Give her some space, but don't give up on her. You both deserve to be happy."

With his last words of wisdom, he leaves my office, closing the door softly for once.

The next few hours, I try and put all the Poppy stuff out of my mind, but it's pointless. She's all I can think about. Shutting down my computer, I decide to go for another run to try and clear my head.

Quickly leaving the gym before anyone can try and speak to me, I take off running toward my parents' house. It's late in the afternoon and the heat from the sun is less intense, but it's still hot as balls out here and I'm soon wiping the sweat from my brow. Turning down the volume on the music blasting in my ears, I try to let the thump of my feet on the road drown out my thoughts. I keep pushing myself faster and faster, but running away from my problems feels like a race I'll never win.

Less than thirty minutes later, I slow down as I approach the street my parents have lived on all my life. Stopping on the small lawn at the front of their house, I do a few stretches to try and cool down my overworked muscles.

"You look like you could use one of these," a familiar voice says from somewhere behind me. Twisting my torso around, I see one of the neighbors out on the porch, with a bottle of water stretched out to me. The smile that stretches across my face feels foreign, but not smiling at Miss Addy is not an option.

She moved in next door to us when I was eleven years old, and her sons and I became great friends. TJ and I spent almost as much time there as we did in our own home. She's a tiny little thing, barely five feet tall. She looks sweet and innocent, but I know from personal experience how scary she can get. There were plenty of times us kids got on the wrong side of her temper.

Stepping into the porch, she pats the seat next to her and I take a seat on the swing. "Thank you," I say, accepting the cold water she hands me.

"So, what's got you frowning so hard?" she asks and, for a second, I contemplate trying to brush her off.

I've talked myself round in circles, trying to decide what to do about Poppy. TJ is always going to be biased about giving me advice, so maybe getting another perspective is what I need. So, I start from the beginning and tell her everything. She already knows how Poppy and I ended on not-so-great terms, but she doesn't know the reasons why, so when she hears me say what really happened, I can tell she's itching to slap me upside my head.

Just like the rest of the people in my life, Addy loved Poppy; they'd bonded over a love of books. Addy owns the small bookstore in town, and I lost count of how much time Poppy would spend in there with her, getting lost in talks of book boyfriends and happily-ever-afters.

I may be an adult now, but the wrath of this woman still frightens the crap out of me as much as it did when I was a kid. I continue on, trying my best to explain how conflicted I am over her being back. By the time I'm finished, the sun has set and the only sound around us is the lawn sprinklers and the chirp of crickets. I'm not used to silence from this woman, and it's making me nervous as all hell.

"Not sure what to make of your silence here." I chuckle nervously.

"That was the biggest load of crap I've ever heard you talk, and that's saying something, considering how much BS you boys talked when you were horny teenagers. You treated that girl like crap. Yes, you were going through a tough time, but that was no excuse for your actions. To top all that off, you just let her walk away from you? I know your mama raised you better than that."

I can't help the laugh that sputters out of me. Good old Addy, being brutally honest as always.

"Stop acting like an overgrown baby and get your girl back."

"You all say that like it's the easiest thing in the world. How do I even start, when she wants me to leave her alone?"

"Since when has love been easy?" she retorts cuttingly. "Loving someone is a full-time job, Keir."

"What if I mess it up? Or let her down again? What if I'm not enough?"

And I realize, as I keep talking, that these are the fears that have been holding me back. What if I'm really just a shitty person that has no business trying to be in a relationship? Is this why I never tried again? If I couldn't get it right for the only person I've ever loved, ever seen a future with, how the hell could I get it right with anyone else?

Addy reaches over and grabs my hand that is now clenched into a tight fist.

"It's ok to be scared of chasing her. It's ok. Being scared just means you're about to do something very brave."

It doesn't feel brave. It feels absolutely terrifying.

Ten

Poppy

"Aunty Poppy, can I haf anuber cookie?" Brooke's cute voice asks from the side of the sun lounger I'm currently seated in.

Elliott and her daughters, Brooke and Bailey, have been here helping me with my garden all morning, and I'm glad for the distraction, even if they are like two little Energizer bunnies. Having two cute four-year-olds running around all day has been exhausting. I have no idea how El does it all *and* manage to keep a smile on her face at all times. Thankfully, the hard work is done and now it's time to relax.

"Ask your momma, sweet girl, she's in the kitchen." I give her a smile as she runs into the house.

Looking around at all the work we've gotten done today, I'm impressed. New flowerbeds and a hammock have made the garden exactly as I wanted it. Frank has had enough of the girls thinking he's their own personal pony, and he's hiding under the tree as far back in the garden as he can get. The early evening sun is still warm, but there's now a gentle breeze that cuts through the muggy air, making it more bearable than it was earlier.

"Drink this and we'll order some dinner. Nobody needs to be cooking after the day we've had." Elliott passes me a cold glass of wine and she sinks into the lounger next to mine. "I totally see why you fell in love with this place."

Her contented sigh mirrors my own. She's right; this place is pretty amazing and the more at home I'm feeling, the more confident I am that I made the right decision to move back.

"The girls are quiet for a minute. Now tell me what's going on with Keir."

There goes my peace and quiet.

"I told you, nothing is going on. He asked me out, I said no, the end."

"The end?"

Rolling my head to face her, I see she's looking at me with a raised eyebrow.

"The. End," I repeat with emphasis.

"I'm not trying to stick my nose in where it isn't wanted, but—"

"But you're going to anyway?" I interrupt on a humorless laugh.

"But I think you're a fool."

Shock has me whipping my head in her direction. "*I'm* a fool?" My voice hits a few octaves higher than normal "Me?! The guy cheated on me, Elliott! Excuse me for being mad." I'm practically shouting now.

"Poppy. I love you, but it was ten years ago…and it was a mistake."

Who is this person and what has she done with my best friend? I can't believe she's saying these things. She was right there with me, she saw the damaged me that was left behind.

"I know it hurt you. You were right to leave him, but that doesn't mean he doesn't deserve another shot. That you *both* don't deserve it." Making sure she has my full attention, she carries on, "People change. None of us are the same people we were back in college."

Not wanting to let her words have any effect on me, I turn away from her intense stare.

"Oh sure, I'll just lay everything on the line, so he can stomp on my heart all over again, shall I?"

Throwing back the full glass of wine, it's empty within a few gulps. I swing my legs off the side of the lounger, about to tell Elliott that it's best she leaves, when I notice she's staring at her own wine glass. Her jaw is set, and I can see it pulse when she squeezes it in frustration. When she raises her eyes to meet mine, they are glassy with unshed tears. I have no idea what has brought this on, but seeing her like this immediately calms my temper.

"Talk to me, El. Tell me what this is really about."

She sighs before turning to me. "I know how hard it was for you then, Pop, but I don't think you realize how hard it's been for me to see you living this half-life ever since."

Her words slam into me, stealing the breath from my chest.

"You always did a good job of pretending. I think you had your brother fooled in the beginning, but I've always been able to see you."

My brain scrambles, trying to come up with some sort of protest. She isn't right. I fought to be me again. I fought damn hard to be happy. I *am* happy. Sure, I'm lonely at times, maybe a little off sometimes, but I'm not unhappy, dammit.

So, why can't I say that then? Why can't I laugh off her words and tell her to stop being ridiculous? It's because my brain won't admit what my heart already knows. I've never gotten over him.

"I'm sorry, but having you back here, getting to seeing you so often. It's too much for me to keep pretending." Elliott keeps talking to me, but I'm stuck inside my own thoughts.

"He let me go, El." It's barely a whisper on the breeze that cuts across my back deck, but she hears it. She hears the thoughts I've kept bottled up since I watched him watch me drive away from Flex. "He let me leave *again*. He doesn't think I'm worth the effort."

The words fall out of my mouth as quietly as the tears that track my face now.

Reaching over, my best friend gathers me into her arms, and all I can think is that it should be Keir holding me, wiping away tears that he's caused yet again.

But it's not. It never is.

The next morning, I wake up with a pounding headache. I'm not sure if it's from the second bottle of wine we drank once the girls went to bed, or from all of the tears I cried. Elliott refused to leave me alone, so we'd had an impromptu sleepover. There's nothing like letting two princess-obsessed four-year-olds give you a makeover to keep the tears at bay for a few hours.

Last night was somewhat of a revelation. I'm not sure where it all came from, but once Elliott opened those floodgates, years' worth of pain came tumbling out. I guess I hadn't moved on quite as much as I thought I had.

Looking at the clock on my bedside table, I see it's almost ten a.m. Judging by the silent house, I'm guessing that Elliott and the girls have already gotten up and left. Shifting out of the bed, I head to the shower to see if I can wash this hangover away.

Once I'm out and dressed in my most comfortable yoga pants and a hoodie, I brave going downstairs to see how much damage we left last night. I distinctly remember us trying to make s'mores while intoxicated.

I expect to see my kitchen looking like a science experiment gone wrong, but I'm delighted to find that everything has been cleared away and my kitchen is spotless. It even smells fresh in here. Thank heavens for best friends.

I'm waiting for the machine to finish making me a coffee when Frank starts barking at the front door, letting me know someone is about to knock. When I swing the door open, I find a young guy standing there, one hand raised ready to knock, and a small bouquet of flowers in the other.

"Miss Nash?" he asks me, looking terrified of Frank, who is standing guard at my side, giving his best mean face.

"That's me."

"These are for you." He almost throws the flowers at me before turning and running down the front steps.

"Stop scaring the people away, Frank," I scold him.

As usual, he ignores me and stalks off, back to the kitchen; looking for food, no doubt. Following behind him, I place the flowers on the kitchen counter and look for a card to see who they are from. They are beautiful. Dusky pink peonies surrounded by creamy soft roses and small wildflowers that I can't name, and they smell heavenly.

Finding the heavy cream envelope nestled in the foliage, I slide the card out and my breath hitches. I'd recognize the scrawl anywhere. There may only be a few words, but that doesn't stop them from making my heart squeeze. The words that, until recently, I didn't think I needed to hear from him.

I'm sorry.

K xo

The sigh that leaves me is a conflicted one. I truly meant it when I asked Keir to leave me alone, but the thrill I feel from him sending me this is undeniable. Bringing the flowers to my face, I breathe in the scent, letting it wash over me. I don't know what the future holds, but I do know that I can't keep hiding from my own feelings any longer.

"So, what did he send today?"

Tucking the phone under my chin, I pick up the small package from the front porch. In the week since the first bunch of flowers were delivered, there's been a gift delivered each day. The day after the first flowers arrived, I'd woken up to another bunch of the same peonies and roses waiting for me perched on top of a small wooden crate. Lifting the lid, I'd been surprised to find two bottles of my favorite Leightons Vineyard wine. The fact he remembered warmed my heart a little. The bottles were nestled in straw, alongside another small envelope. That time, the card simply read,

Keir, x

The third morning, I'd found yet another bouquet. This time, the flowers were inside a huge wicker basket. When I'd taken it inside, I'd found it was filled with fresh pastries and gourmet coffee from the small café we used to go to before classes. For the first time in forever, the rush of nostalgia didn't sting quite so badly.

The flowers and gifts have been waiting for me every morning. Each gift has been a small reminder of happy times in our past. Cupcakes from my favorite bakery, a voucher for the same spa as he'd gotten me for my twentieth birthday. Each time, there has been a card with only his name on it.

"How do you know there was anything there this morning?"

"Because he isn't going to stop chasing you already, that's how I know. Just hurry up and open it."

"Stop being nosy."

I place the newest flowers into a water jug—I ran out of vases after the first few days—and take the parcel with me to sit on the back porch. "I knew I shouldn't have told you about them in the first place."

"Don't be mean. I'm married with kids, I need to get my kicks wherever I can these days. Just hurry up and open the damn thing."

Pulling on the black ribbon, I unravel it and remove the white cardboard lid. Resting on the top of the black tissue paper is another card; this time, it's slightly bigger. Picking it up, I hesitate to read it. For so long, I've kept so much of the past locked away, the good memories hurt more than the bad ones sometimes, but these trips down memory lane have hurt less than anticipated.

Flipping over the note, the words make me catch my breath.

Staying away isn't an option this time.

Be ready at 7 p.m.

K x

"What is it?"

Hearing Elliott whisper through the phone makes me jump; I completely forgot she was there. I read the note out loud to her and she's silent.

"What? Why aren't you saying anything?" Her non-response is making me worried, she always has an opinion on everything.

"I think he just swooned me into silence."

I roll my eyes at her comment. "Is that all it takes? Pete must really be slacking in the romance skills these days," I scoff.

"Let's not even go there." She shuts me down, and I make a mental note to come back to her comment later. There's been a few times too many she's alluded to her and her husband having issues lately. "What's in the box?"

I put the phone on speaker and place it next to the box, so I can open it with both hands. Shifting the tissue paper, I pick up what is obviously a smaller-sized hardcover book. Lifting the book out, I see it's a copy of my favorite book, *Jane Eyre*.

"Oh shit!" I gasp as I take in the worn cover with the edges slightly bent, the beautiful embossed flowers are faded, but still spectacular. It's an old copy but still in amazing condition. Gently opening the front cover, I find yet another card. When I read it, the tears that had been gently filling my eyes spill over. He's quoted one of my favorite lines from the book.

I never meant to wound you thus...Will you ever forgive me?

Staying strong against Keir's advances just got a whole lot harder.

Eleven

Keir

Placing the box and flowers down gently on Poppy's porch, I move back down the steps. I only get a few steps when I see movement at the window. Like clockwork, a huge dog's head pops up, shifting the blinds to get a better look at me. He has done this every morning this week when I've snuck up leave things for Poppy. He is a monster of a dog, and I have no idea what breed it is, but he's huge and scary as fuck. He's got to be at least one hundred pounds of muscle and fur. I expected him to bark when he saw me the first time, but all I'd gotten was a head tilt and a hard stare. I've no idea how someone as feminine as Poppy ended up with this beast for a pet.

Quickly getting into the truck I parked a few doors down, and driving away, I have to fight the urge to turn around and go knock her door. I wish I could be there when she opens the gifts I've been leaving. Has she liked them? Did they mean anything to her? Did she understand what they meant to me. It's only gotten harder and harder to leave her place every time I've been here.

After my talk with Addy last week, I'd wracked my brain trying to come up with ways to show her that I might be physically giving her space, but I had no intention of making that space permanent. Her favorite wine was easy to find, and the breakfast basket was a simple reminder of a time when things were good. Well, at least I hoped she had good memories of that time. I sure as fuck did, and I wanted her to remember those more than the shitty ones that came after.

Pulling into my parking space at Flex, I make my way inside with a bounce in my step that's been missing lately. I'm nervous about the last gift I just left with Poppy, but I have a good feeling about it. I'm almost certain she'll agree to meet with me tonight. I've had plenty of time to think all this shit through, and TJ was right about one thing. When I'd walked her to her door that night last week, there was definitely something there. I'm pretty sure she still has at least some sort of feelings for me. I'd had to battle with myself not to drag her into my arm and kiss the shit out of her.

The thought of seeing her again later has me pumped, and I greet the staff standing in reception with a smile. I must have been even moodier than I thought lately, judging by the surprised looks I get as I pass by. Lucy is waiting for me in my office when I get there, and she does not look happy at all.

"Everything ok?" I ask, stupidly it would seem, judging by how hard she just slammed down the phone she was using onto the glass desk top.

"Steph quit. Again!" she shouts. "Tell your damn brother that if you guys want to keep any of the decent female trainers around here, to keep his junk zipped up."

TJ isn't a fan of the "non-fraternization" style of running a business. He's gotten it on with more of the staff than I care to think of. Steph is one of our best trainers, and has had a crush on TJ since she started here a year ago. Doesn't matter how many times he was warned she's not the "one-night stand" kind of girl, TJ couldn't resist. He's already had to sweet talk her into coming back to work after she quit the last two times he left her bed and jumped straight into someone else's.

"I'll speak to him." I sigh as I drop into my chair "What else do we have on today?" I ask, trying to defuse some of the tension in the room.

Lucy was never supposed to be my assistant, but we were so in over our heads those first few months after we opened, she stepped up and gradually started doing more and more of our admin stuff, alongside running her own classes. She's been with us since before we opened this place, and I would be lost without her insane organizational skills. She keeps slamming things into the filing cabinet as she gives me a rundown of the appointments I have today.

"Are you ok?" I ask.

"Fine," she snaps, but doesn't lift her head. She just carries on, moving shit around as if it really needs to be organized.

"Luce?" I try and get her to stop, but she barely even registers I'm talking. "Stop!"

My shout gets her to lift her eyes to me and immediately I can tell she's on the verge of tears. Her eyes are red-rimmed and her lips are trembling with the effort it's taking her not to cry.

"What's wrong?" I ask, moving toward her.

"Nothing." She puts her hand up to stop me before I get to her. "I must be hormonal or something."

She tries to brush me off, knowing that any mention of hormones will shut me up. I'm not buying it though, but after staring at her a beat, I decide not to push her.

"I'm fine. I promise." The smile she gives is weak but before I can push her any further, the door to my office opens again and TJ barges in. He's messing with the phone in his hands and doesn't bother to look up before dropping into the chair in front of my desk.

"Bro, remind me to listen to you next time you tell me not to bang the staff. Steph might be wild in the sack, but no pussy is worth the days of shit that come after it."

I don't get a chance to answer before Lucy is slamming the drawer shut.

"What's wrong, T? She pissed you left her with an STD? Must have been a doozy to cause her to quit again." She bites out the words with so much venom, they almost make me shrink back in my chair. Keeping my eyes on TJ, I see him squeeze his own shut. His back is to her, so she can't see the color drain from his face, or how he cringes at the sound of her voice.

"I'm taking a personal day, I suddenly feel sick to my stomach. Your schedule is up to date, and the stuff you ordered for tonight has been delivered as you asked.”

Yanking her bag out from under the chair in the corner of the room, she storms out without a backwards glance. TJ lets his head drop back on his shoulders, and a pained groan escapes.

“Nice one. You could have warned me she was in here.” He shoots me a glare.

“Maybe you could try not being a dickhead once in a while, and you wouldn’t offend pretty much every female you meet.” I’m shocked to see a look of hurt cross his face at my words. “What's going on with you two?”

“Me and who?”

“Don't play dumb, T.” I’ve no idea where this animosity between them has sprung from. As far as I know, he and Lucy have never been anything more than friends.

“Long story”—he sighs—“and not one I want to start without at least a few beers in hand. Maggie’s tonight? I’ll call the guys.”

Just the mention of tonight makes my stomach clench. I’m so fucking nervous.

“Can we do it another night? I have plans,” I say, while keeping my eyes on the screen in front of me, not wanting TJ to see my face. I’ve not told him or anyone else, except for Addy, about my plan.

“You never have plans. What's going on?”

“I do so have plans. You don't know everything,” I huff. Apparently, we’re still a pair of kids.

“Spill it, little bro. Did you finally give in to that chick from the sports drink people?”

“Fuck no, I told you that's never happening. She’s got bigger balls than the both of us.” One of the reps we get our stock from has never been shy about propositioning me whenever she’s here, and doesn’t understand the word no.

Deciding just to go for it, I tell him all about the stuff I’ve been sending to Poppy and my plans for tonight.

“Damn,” he says when I’m done, and the grin on his face is huge. “You got this, brother. There’s no way she’ll be able to resist you after this.”

“You think so?” I’m praying he’s right.

“I know so. And if there’s one thing I know, it’s how to woo a woman.”

“Judging by the fact that one of our best girls quit today, and Lucy can't stand the sight of you, I’d say you’ve still got some shit to learn in the *wooing* department.”

“Fuck you. I’ll get back on Steph’s good side by the end of the day, just you wait and see.”

I don't doubt for a minute that he’ll make good on that promise. It also doesn’t escape me that he doesn’t include Lucy in it.

The rest of the day passes by in a blur of staff meetings and training sessions. No matter how busy I've been, my thoughts have never been far from Poppy, and how she'll react to tonight. I'm aware that I've arranged a date based on what the Poppy I used to know would like. I have no idea what she's been up to since I saw her last. Does she still like the same things?

After stepping out of the shower and drying myself quickly, I throw on jeans and a shirt. Now that most of the day has flown by, I'm suddenly staring at the clock, willing it to move faster so I can leave already. I need to know if she's going to agree to this or slam the door in my face.

Parking the truck outside the house this time, I make my way up the porch again for the second time today, and there's no sign of the dog this time. I have to wipe the palms of my hands on my jeans before I knock, then I hear the tap of paws coming toward the door and Poppy telling the dog to move out of her way.

The door swings open, and there she is, looking so beautiful I forget to breathe for a second.

Poppy

"I'm telling you, this is a bad idea." Pacing around my bedroom, I start jamming all the cosmetics I've just used back into the bag. "You know we have these gut instincts for a reason. I would be insane to ignore it, right?"

Frank lifts his head from the bed for a second before flopping back down with a loud huff.

"You know I'm right," I babble on to him. Sipping the large glass of wine, I wonder to myself just how suspicious it would look if I suddenly came down with a 'mystery illness'? Or maybe I can say I fell down and broke a limb? Anything to get out of tonight's date.

Date? Is that even what this is? Do you go on a date with someone you used to love? Oh shit, *it is a date*. With Keir. The man who broke me once before.

Who the hell thought that was a good idea? Urgh, just thinking about it has my anxiety levels rising.

Rushing over to my phone, I call Elliott for moral support. It doesn't even ring once before she answers.

"*You are going!*" is shouted in my ear before I get a single word out. Dammit.

"But why?" I whine into the phone like a brat. "I really don't think I'm ready for this yet."

I love my best friend, I really, really do, but right now, I don't exactly like her for talking me into doing this. Standing in front of the floor-length mirror in my closet, I yank on one of the curls that hang down over my chest. I've spent a lot of time and effort to look like I *haven't* made any effort for tonight.

I can't help but wonder what Keir sees when he looks at me now. My once long dark hair has been highlighted for years now, the blonde another attempt at trying to find a 'new me,' and I've curled and teased it to look like I just rolled out of bed. I'm wearing ripped jeans and a tight black, long-sleeved bodysuit. I've thrown on my white Chucks, hoping they make me look like I'm not trying too hard. Finally, I grab a jacket to take with me.

"Remember what I said earlier?" Elliott says in my ear. "Just go, listen to what he has to say, and if you're not feeling it, you never have to see him again."

After we both stay silent for a beat, she adds, "Don't live another day with regrets, Lolly-pop."

Oh shit. She must be serious if she's busting out my old nickname.

"El…" I start to say, but she cuts me off.

“Trust me, Pop, the fear you’re feeling? That *will* pass, no matter the outcome of tonight. But the regrets of not giving it a shot? Those will stay forever.”

She’s obviously talking from experience and my heart breaks for my best friend. She’s been getting quieter and more withdrawn as the days pass. I wish she’d just tell me what's going on with her. But she’s right. I have a feeling I’ll always regret not taking this chance.

“I’ll make a deal with you. I’ll go and listen to what he has to stay, if you promise me you’ll stop pretending everything is ok.”

The silence from the other end of the line is thick. I hear a small sniffle that tells me she’s crying.

“Deal,” she whispers before quickly saying her goodbyes.

Now that she’s gone, the nerves are back in full force. I just need this night to be over. I’m going to hear him out, then hopefully I’ll be able to move on. Really move on this time.

What the heck are we even doing this for? Surely the past is best left behind us? Keir cheated on me. I learned to accept the hurt his actions caused, and I eventually felt like I had moved on, but I’ve never forgiven him. Is that something I’ll ever be able to do? I’m hoping so because moving here and seeing him again has shown me exactly how much I’ve been living in limbo. Never letting anyone get too close because I never wanted to be hurt that way again. Maybe forgiving him will close that chapter once and for all.

I've gotten through the day by blocking all thoughts of Keir from my mind. I've taken Frank for a long walk, cleaned the whole house, and even sorted through thousands of unread emails. Now I'm watching the minutes creep closer to seven p.m., and I'm powerless to stop the thoughts invading my mind.

Pouring myself a second glass of wine for courage, I sit on the back steps, looking out at the small garden that's become my safe haven of sorts. Taking a few deep breaths, I rest my head on the wooden railings and close my eyes. Images of Keir flash through my mind. Images of the boy that swept me off my feet flicker alongside images of the man he is now, still so damn handsome. Butterflies take flight in my belly at the thought of him. Butterflies. It's been a long ass time since I've felt those.

I'm pulled from my thoughts when Frank moves through the kitchen behind me and walks toward the front door, the tap of his paws the only sound on the quiet evening air. Looking at the time on my phone, I see there's still almost forty minutes until Keir is due to be here, but I'm too nervous to sit here and continue to overthink this.

Finishing up the last of the wine, I make my way inside to make sure everything is locked up before I leave. I stop when I notice that Frank is just sitting in the middle of the hallway, staring at the closed front door. I jump when there's a loud knock in the door, but the dog just continues to sit and stare. For the first time ever, he's not barking like a crazy thing.

Shooing him out the way, I pull the door open without bothering to check who it is. My heart leaps into my throat when my eyes land on Keir, standing there on my doorstep. How is it that I've memorized every single part of this man, yet I'm still struck dumb every time I see him? He's just wearing his usual outfit, jeans and a Henley shirt, and his dark hair pokes out of the bottom of the worn Fury cap he's wearing, but somehow, he looks utterly perfect.

"Hi." His smile is a little hesitant, almost as if he's not sure of the reception he was going to get from me. The fact that he isn't sure of himself is totally endearing.

"Hey, you're early," I reply, and he at least looks a little sheepish at this, reaching back to scratch his neck quickly. The move reminds me of the other first date we had. He'd been nervous then too, and I'd found it cute as hell.

"Yeah, I guess my patience level is pretty low today." He chuckles, and it breaks a little of the tension cloud we've been standing in. "It's been a long week."

"It's been an interesting one, that's for sure." We both chuckle now, before falling into an awkward silence.

"Thank you—"

"So I—"

We both start at to speak at the same time, and again, there is that dreaded awkward laugh.

"I was just going to say thank you for the flowers and stuff. Everything was incredibly thoughtful."

Keir gives me bigger smile this time, and I can't help but drop my eyes to his full lips. The way they spread wider with the smile, showing the barest hint of the dimples that only come out when he really laughs. The smile looks almost rusty, like he's not used to it being on his face.

Letting my eyes flick back up to his, I see some of the tension ease out of him, only to have it replaced with something that looks a lot like longing. He keeps looking at me, and I can't help but stare back, completely aware that this is odd behavior, but still powerless to stop it.

Finally shaking myself out of it, I realize we're still standing in the doorway. I need a minute away from him. Not even five minutes around him, and my brain is already short-circuiting.

"I'm sorry, please come in while I get the dog settled so we can leave." I move back and wave my hand for him to come inside. "I won't keep you long."

Nodding his head, he follows me as I point to the kitchen, and tell him to help himself to a drink.

"I'll be right back," I say as I rush into the bathroom, cursing the fact I'm wearing makeup because all I want to do right now is splash cold water over myself. Anything to get rid of the blush Keir has just caused to erupt all over me. How in the hell is it possible to still be so affected by him after all this time apart? I should hate him, shouldn't I? Seems my body disagrees.

"Get it together," I whisper to myself forcefully as I quickly brush my teeth.

Once I'm feeling a little more put together, I make my way back out to where I left Keir standing. As I walk over to where he is, I notice that Frank is standing next to him. How odd. Frank never lets people come into the house without at least a few barks; usually there's a few growls thrown in for good measure. Kier is absently scratching his head while he looks at the wall of photographs in my hallway.

"What kind of dog is he?"

I'm so lost in my own thoughts that I missed Kier walking toward me.

"Oh, he's a Newfie. Probably mixed with something else, though. I got him at the pound and they said he was found in a dumpster, along with five other puppies." Calling Frank away, I tell him to get on his dog bed, knowing full well that I'll come home to find him in my bed later, waiting for me.

"He's usually a much better guard dog than he was tonight, though," I say, as we walk out of the house.

"He's probably just used to me by now."

"Why would he be used to you?" I ask, confused as to why he would think that.

"He's been watching me drop of packages off on your doorstep all week, so…" He trails off.

I don't know which thought to process first; the fact that he's put so much effort into his gifts or the fact that my dog has not barked at him once in the last week. I don't have the mental capacity to deal with being this close to Keir and my dog's strange behavior, so instead of dwelling, I file it all away in my mind to pour over later. Preferably with Elliott and a bottle of tequila.

Opening the truck door for me, Keir puts his hand on the small of my back while he helps me up into the seat. His touch is brief, but the thrill it leaves on my skin is not.

Thirteen

Keir

Thankfully the drive I have planned is short, because the silence here in the cab is deafening. All week, I've had this idea that I'd give her this perfect night. Wine and dine her. Show her I'm still the same guy she was with before. No, not the same—*better*. I just didn't anticipate how goddamned awkward it would be. We don't know each other anymore, but we're not strangers. Making small talk about the weather and work seems trivial, but how do you talk about the last ten years without addressing the reasons for the distance between us?

I didn't think this thing through properly, and now I'm freaking the fuck out. Did I really think we could just pick up where we left off? By the time I pull up outside Addy's bookstore, I'm seriously considering taking Poppy home and forgetting I ever had this stupid idea.

Once we park, I tell her to wait there. I can't take her inside like I planned to; just thinking about the romantic picnic I have set up in there makes me cringe. Instead, I help her out of the truck and walk us across the road and into the park. It's still warm and sunny, the park still busy with kids playing and people walking their dogs. Seeing an empty bench, I sit, gesturing for Poppy to follow me.

"I'm sorry."

I can feel her look at me, but I keep my eyes forward. It's easier to talk when I'm not getting lost in how beautiful she is.

"What for?" she asks. As if she doesn't know.

"This. Asking you to do this when you were clear you wanted to be left alone," I say. "I got caught up in planning this night without considering how weird it might be."

"It *is* weird, huh?" she laughs. Turning to look at her, I can't help but laugh too. She always did have the innate ability to make everything seem ok, even when it wasn't.

"Just a little." I look back out at someone pushing their kid on a swing. "I just thought if I could get you to spend some time with me…"

I trail off because I don't even know what I was thinking, and I don't know how to explain to her that the first time I saw her again, all I could think of was making her mine. How do I tell her that all I've thought about is kissing her? About holding her as close as I possibly can and tasting those lips, the ones that have haunted me for years now. How do I say that I've done nothing but dream of her? Not just getting her back under me, but having her surrounding me, in every aspect of my life. Because that's all I want. I want to be with her in all ways, at all times. Trying to convey that without sounding like a crazy stalker is beyond me right now.

Taking yet another deep breath, I try again, shifting on the bench so I'm facing her. "I guess I just didn't think. I was being selfish. But now that I have you here, I'd really like to just forget the whole date thing."

For a second, I swear I see disappointment on her face, but it clears quickly as I continue. "How about we grab some food instead? Catch up on what you've been up to for the last ten years?"

I hold my breath while I wait for her reply, and I'm so fucking relieved when she smiles at me softly.

"I think that sounds perfect."

After the awkward beginning to the night, we've had a surprisingly good time. We ate burgers as she told me all about her life, traveling from city to city. I've told her about my time playing football and starting up Flex with TJ, and how my family is doing. It's turned out to be an incredibly relaxing evening.

The one thing we haven't talked about is our shared history. The time we were together and how it ended. I don't think either of us wants to disturb the fragile ground we're on right now. I'm just enjoying the time with her.

Just as we're getting ready to leave, someone approaches the table and asks me for an autograph for their kids. It hardly ever happens anymore, but often enough that I still try to wear a cap or sunglasses when I go out. Smiling through a selfie and a couple of signed napkins, I glance over at Poppy to see that she's deep in thought. When we leave the bar, she's still quiet.

"I'm sorry about that, it never really happens anymore. Not since I stopped playing."

She stops walking and turns to look at me.

"Don't ever apologize for the success you had. No matter what, be proud of everything you achieved."

I know she's right, and it's not that I'm not proud, but my playing pro was ultimately what caused us to fall apart. I can accept responsibility for my actions, but even before that, the tension that being apart for so long caused was picking at the seams of us. I don't want to throw it in her face, but I should have known she wouldn't dwell on the negatives like that.

The urge to kiss her is bordering on uncontrollable, so I do the only thing possible in that moment. I bite my cheek and pray that I can keep a lid on it for a while longer.

When we continue walking, she asks me if this was what I originally planned for tonight.

"Definitely not," I answer on a laugh. "Let's just say my plans were a lot more cheesy than this."

"Tell me," she says with a grin, bumping her shoulder against my arm. The sparks that are always present when she touches me flare to life.

"Oh no. we've had a great night, I'm not ending it with you laughing at me."

"Why would I laugh?" She turns her head slightly to face me and once again, my breath disappears at the sight of her. She steals all the air from my lungs whenever I get a glimpse of her. God, what I wouldn't do to freeze this moment. Her standing close enough to touch, the evening sun long since set, leaving the bright moon to cast pale light down on her. She's perfect.

"Let's just say that it was completely the wrong first date to plan for our situation."

Her breath catches on the word date, and I'm worried I've spooked her. I'm right that my original plan would have backfired spectacularly, though. Romantic picnic and candles would have had her running a mile from me. I should have known that casual would be the best way to go with Poppy. After a beat of silence, she lets go of whatever was bothering her. We keep walking back in the direction of my truck, side by side. She's close enough to touch and it's bordering on impossible not to reach down and take a hold of her hand each time it brushes against me.

"I'll get you to tell me one day." She laughs, and I resist doing a fist pump over the fact she's just basically said we'll be seeing each other again.

"Maybe one day I'll show you." I hold my breath, hoping again that I've not pushed too far.

She doesn't make me wait too long before she replies quietly, "Maybe."

The rest of the walk passes in silence, but it's a comfortable one this time. When we get the corner of the block, the sound of a guitar starts up. There's a group of teenagers in the park sitting on the benches where we sat earlier; one has a beat up old acoustic guitar in his hands and another starts to sing along. When I hear the words of the song being sung, I reach down and grab Poppy's hand. She lets out a small gasp at the contact, and I gently tug her hand to stop her walking.

"Dance with me?"

"What?" Her mouth drops open as she gasps out a laugh; she's so fucking cute.

"Come on, I love this song."

I don't give her time to say no, quickly stepping up to her and wrapping my hands around her waist. I lift her a few inches off the floor, then place her back down gently with her tiny feet on top of mine. I move one arm around her waist to hold her close to me, as the other takes one of her hands and brings it to rest on my chest. She's frozen, locked in place, and I pray she doesn't bolt. I know I'm being bold as fuck, but it just feels right.

"You…you…" She stumbles over whatever she's trying to say.

"Shhh...just listen," I whisper into her ear.

When she hears the words of the song, she drops my hand and moves both arms up around my neck. They sing about a man doing anything he can to get his love to come back to him. About the lengths he'd go to repair the damage he caused. She turns her face in toward my neck, and her nose brushes against me. My legs almost buckle under the weight of the feelings that small movement sends rushing through me. She feels so perfect here, in my arms. I've missed her of course, but this feeling? It's like coming home.

I continue to sway us slowly side to side as the song goes on. I have no idea if I'm doing the right thing, but the moment feels so right, so perfect, that I can't help myself. I need her to know that I might have allowed tonight to be more about two friends reconnecting than anything romantic, but want I her back. I'm not giving up. Not again.

"I remember that day," I say, just loud enough for her to hear. "I remember all the days."

Her arms squeeze me gently so I know she's hearing me. She doesn't need to ask what day I'm talking about. We had only been dating for a few weeks and I'd taken her to the beach. I was supposed to be studying for a test, so I'd taken some textbooks and Poppy took her kindle. We spent an afternoon, lying there in the sun, just being us. No forced conversation, no awkward silences. It was one of the reasons I'd known I wanted more with her; that feeling of being completely at ease when we were together was intoxicating to me.

Despite knowing I needed to study, I spent more time watching Poppy than anything else, so when a tear fell from her eyes, I'd noticed it right away. When she explained that she was crying because the guy in her book had let his girl dance on his feet, and that's what her dead father used to do, I put my own book down and kissed her. Then I'd laid back on the blanket with her head in my lap and had her read the rest of the book to me out loud. It's one of my favorite memories of us, the simplicity of the moment epitomizing everything I loved about us as a couple.

We stay like this, her in my arms, gently swaying for the longest time, both lost in memories. Until her tears dry, and the music stops.

Poppy

I remember...

Three days later, and those words still have the same effect on me as they did when he whispered them in my ear. When Keir had asked me to dance with him, right there in the park, I'd thought he was kidding. Until he'd started swaying us and I'd become engulfed in memories, that is.

I've had that whole night on repeat in my mind in the days that have passed. From the moment I opened the door and saw him standing there, to how my heart had dropped into my stomach when he'd said to forget about going on a date. As much as I'd tried to convince myself that I agreed to go out with him to get closure, I have to admit that I'd secretly been thinking of it as a real date.

I've done nothing but stare at my laptop screen for at least the last hour, my mind full of conflict over Keir. My thoughts are like a pendulum, swinging wildly between wanting him one minute to wanting him out of my life for good the next. Maybe we've had our time?

Maybe we were always destined to be an incomplete sentence. An unfinished chapter in my life story.

Or maybe there is more to come for us.

For once, I'm grateful for the ringing of my phone; the distraction from myself is much needed. Picking up my cell phone, I see it's my brother calling. I've not spoken to him in a few weeks. When he signed up for the military, neither of us thought he'd make a career out of it, but he did.

Growing up, it was pretty much always just Duke and I. We never knew our dad and our mom just wasn't around. She was never mean or cruel to us, we never went without the material things. The only thing we lacked was a parent that was present in our lives. At three years older than me, my brother took on that role. He was the one who helped with homework, listened to me cry over bitchy schoolgirls, and stupid teenage boy drama. He was my rock. Still is, in a lot of ways. My relationship with my mother is now nonexistent. The only contact is the odd Christmas card that arrives in the mail some years.

"Hey, Duke!" I answer excitedly.

"Dimples, it's so good to hear your voice."

I'm so happy to hear from him, I let the stupid nickname slide. "Where are you?"

"Still overseas, but I just heard we'll be back stateside soon. This time, I'm thinking of staying a while. Until the Army says otherwise, of course."

I'm giddy with excitement at hearing this; we only see each other a few times a year. Between my constant moving around, and his back-to-back deployments, we just haven't had much luck. We chat for a few minutes about my move back to Savannah and everything that's gone on with Elliott, and I skillfully manage to hide that fact that I've been in turmoil over the whole Keir situation. At least I hope I have.

"Pop, I don't have long to chat but before I go, I need to know you're ok."

"Why wouldn't I be?" I try to keep my voice even, but I'm not sure it's working.

"Don't be a brat. I know it wasn't easy to go back there. It wasn't easy for me either, you know?"

I do know. Duke has always been a "fixer," and it must have torn him apart to be so far away from me.

"Have you seen him yet?"

I really should lie and tell him no. I shouldn't burden him with any of my crap, but lying to my brother is something I've never done.

"Yep," I answer, "and before you try and hop a plane home to look after me, I'm perfectly fine."

The huff of air through the phone is enough to tell me how hard Duke is working to keep his anger in. "Tell me what happened, Pop, from the beginning. I have time."

And so I do. I tell him about the first time I saw Keir again. I tell him about the flowers and notes. I tell him about a beautiful evening with the man that once broke my heart, and finally, I tell him about this bone-deep feeling I have that Keir and I are not at the end of our story yet. He lets out a pained sigh before he speaks again.

"It kills me to say this to my baby sister, but you only get one chance at living. I wish I could tell you to forget he even exists, but I can't. Elliott is right, for once. You need to put whatever is holding you back aside for a minute and take a chance. Go get your happy back."

I should have known that Duke would put my feelings over his own dislike of Keir. I don't think he's ever gotten over the urge to beat the shit out of him.

"I'll think about it, Duke. Pinky promise." I can hear the guys with Duke get louder, so I say my goodbyes. "Love you, be safe, and send me the details for when you get home. You can stay here with me."

"Will do." After a second of silence, he says, "Look after *you*, Poppy. Just be careful, yeah? For me?"

"Yeah, Duke. I can do that for you," I whisper, tears making my voice hoarse.

When we hang up, I allow myself a few minutes to cry. No matter how long he's been an Army Ranger, I still worry about him.

After I finally pull myself together and freshened up, I grab my keys and Frank's leash, then head out to Deja Brew to get a well-deserved coffee.

I swing the door open, but stop short when I see Keir leaning one of his hands against the doorframe, the other raised as if he's about to knock. His head is bowed, that dark hair a wild mess on his head. Before I can ask him what he's doing here, he looks up at me. When our eyes meet, I'm floored by the look he gives me, and the chaos that swirls behind them.

With one step toward me, his big, safe, strong hands reach up and cup my face. There are no words exchanged before his lips crash down onto mine.

Keir

Pacing back and forth along Poppy's porch, I ask myself what the fuck I'm doing here, for the tenth time since I jumped into my truck and drove over here. After three days of listening to TJ tell me to follow "the plan," I couldn't take it anymore. I hadn't planned on staying away from her, but I'd been incredibly turned on from being so close to her all night, I left quickly before I did something stupid, like drag her into her house and into the nearest bed.

I'd had a semi all night from being next to her. Hell, just holding her hand on the way to the truck was almost enough to push me over the edge.

"Four days is nothing. Give it a week and then you can call her."

My brother's voice echoes through my mind but I hadn't been able to last the rest of the day, let alone the rest of the week. Not without at least speaking to Poppy.

So here I am, wondering what the hell I'm going to say to her. How I'm going to convince her to take a chance on me again. Just as I'm about to knock the door, it swings open. Poppy stands there, Frank by her side, with his leash on and his tail wagging. When I look up to her, words escape me. Need takes over and my body gives into what it's been craving for weeks now. Gently taking her face in my hands, I don't hesitate anymore. I catch the shocked gasp that tumbles from her lips with my own.

When our lips meet, it's not *just* a kiss.

The room falls away as I get lost in this embrace, lost in her.

There is a calmness in this moment that washes over me, touching me everywhere, until Poppy lets out the smallest of sighs against my lips. It's like a lit match igniting the tiny sliver of space left between us. My tongue seeks entry past her lips as I pull her closer still. I can't get her close enough to me; the feel of my skin touching hers isn't even enough right now. My heart misses a beat as I realize this is what I've been waiting for.

This moment, with this woman, is why nothing in my life has felt right for the longest time.

We stand there, in her foyer, and I don't know if minutes have passed, or hours. All I know is the feel of her lips on mine and the glide of her tongue against mine. She kisses me back with a heat that matches my own, her hands twisted tightly at the back of my shirt, like she's scared I'll let go. My own hands slide from where they cradle her face, down the smooth skin of her shoulders, gradually making it to her waist. Gripping her hips, I lift her up, and she wraps her legs around me.

We still fit together like two puzzle pieces. Kicking the door shut, I move us into the room, toward the sofa, managing to sit down without breaking the kiss. Slowing the movement of my lips on hers, I keep her straddling my lap. The heat of her against my hard-on is a special kind of torture.

Moving my head back slightly, I watch her eyes flutter open. The hazel pools swirling underneath heavy lids are more of a liquid green, and I remember that used to happen when she was turned on. The sight makes my blood sing.

"Hi."

"Hi," she whispers back shyly. "That was some hello," and her words make us both smile.

"I probably should apologize, but to be honest, I've been wanting to do that since the first moment I saw you again. I should be congratulated for being able to restrain myself till now."

She looks at me with soft eyes, a blush stealing its way over her cheeks. She squirms on my lap, making me groan at the contact.

"I'm sorry." She blushes even harder when she notices the bulge pressing into her.

Gripping her hips, I pull her back down on my lap, burying my face into her neck and letting out a groan. Fuck, she feels good. She's stiff for a second before her hands move to the back of my head, holding me against her. Her heartbeat thumps, fast and strong against mine. When our breathing slows, she slides off my lap and sits to my side, still close but not close enough. I know there a thousand things I need to say, but I still take a second to revel in the feelings being with her brings out in me.

"I want another chance," I say, smashing the silence between us to bits. The conflict I see on her face doesn't surprise me, but still hurts. I need her to want this as much as I do.

"I don't know, Keir. There's so much history between us…"

"Just a chance, that's all I need," I interrupt whatever she was about to say. Placing a hand on her chin, I stop her from turning away from me. I want her to be able to see the sincerity on my face. "I was an idiot, but I know what I lost, Poppy. I would never ask if I didn't think we could be something."

She keeps her eyes on mine and I can see her warring with herself. All I can do is pray. Pray she's brave enough to try.

"I'm not her," she says timidly, her words confusing me.

"Who?"

"I'm not the same girl I was. I'm not her."

Guilt slices through me at the reminder of how much I hurt her.

“That’s ok. I’m not the same guy I was then either,” I say on a sigh. “I’m not asking to pick up where we left off. I’m asking for a chance to find out who we both are now, to find out who we could maybe be together.”

Her eyes drop to my chest, where her fingers are tracing the Flex logo on my shirt. The contact soothes me in a way she wouldn’t understand. When she stays silent, I keep pressing on.

“I broke us.” Her surprised eyes fly up to meet mine. “I broke you, and now I want a chance to fix it. Fix us.”

I don't know what she’s looking for as she continues to silently stare at me, but she must find it because she leans forward and brushes her swollen lips over mine. This kiss might lack the heat of the one that came before it, but it’s the most important one of my life so far.

“Ok.”

The word spoken against my lips, as light as a feather, would be enough to bring me to my knees if I was standing.

Sixteen

Poppy

Keir- Text me when you get here.

I stare at the phone in my hand. I don't bother replying that I've already been outside of Flex for the last five minutes. Letting my guard down and allowing Keir back in wasn't a difficult choice after I felt his lips on mine. I'd been on the cusp of admitting that to myself, but that kiss? Well, that had proven to me that whatever was still there between us, was more than worth pursuing. That doesn't mean I'm not scared out of my mind.

After his declaration, we spent the rest of the evening making out like a pair of horny teenagers. Frank never got his walk, but the grin that had taken up residence on my face made any guilt vanish. I have no doubt I'm making the right choice by letting him back in. Elliott's words have been ringing through my mind. I *have* kept my guard up for so long, honestly thinking it would protect me from getting hurt, but it came at a cost. One that was steeper than even I had realized. I know I would always regret it if I don't take this chance. Over the last few days, there have been a lot of text messages and late-night phone calls, but this will be the first time I've seen him in person since then.

So why am I sitting outside, instead of going in to meet him like planned? I wish I knew. I guess old habits die hard and a part of me is stuck in self-preservation mode. As much as I want to throw caution to wind and forget the past, that's just not me. Not yet anyway.

I'm about to type out a text to tell him I'm here when there's a knock at my window, causing me to jump right out of my seat. With my hand over my heart, I turn to see Lucy grinning at me through the window. Pushing my door open, I step out of my car and lock it up.

"I'm so sorry!" she says brightly. "I didn't mean to scare you."

"Don't worry at all." I smile back at her, even though my nerves are frayed.

"Are you here for one of the classes? I was hoping you'd be back," she asks, as we walk toward the entrance to the gym.

I pull at the hem of the denim shorts I have on. When I'd woken up to a text from Keir, asking me to meet him here after work, I'd spent hours deciding what to wear. He asked me to the gym; does that mean he wants to work out? Or is it date, and should I dress cute? After spending way too long deciding, I'd settled on short shorts and a shirt, rolling the sleeves up to make the outfit more casual, figuring he would have told me if we were going anywhere that needed me to dress up.

"Actually, no," I say nervously. "I'm here to meet someone."

"Keir?" She smirks at me. I'm not surprised she knows that, I don't think I did a good job at hiding just how well we knew each other last time I was here.

"Yes, actually." I laugh, rubbing my damp palms over my shorts.

"Hmm, that explains the sudden good mood then." It warms something in me to think that us reconnecting has him happy too. "Come on, I'll take you to him."

She swings the glass door open, letting me walk in ahead of her. It's much busier in here than it was last time I was here. As we walk through the main floor, I see that almost all the bikes are full and there are groups of people around most of the weight machines. The music is loud, but it doesn't drown out the clunks and bangs of the equipment.

Lucy continues to make small talk as we make our way to what I'm guessing is Keir's office. I'm sure she's doing it to distract me from the stares I'm getting. I'm thinking that my outfit choice was probably not the best; I stick out like a sore thumb. The stares only get worse when we make it down to the basement. Down here, there are less people, and the few that are there are in one of the boxing rings that are set up. Two guys are wearing head protection as they throw punches at each other. The others in there with them stop watching the fighters and instead turn to where Lucy and I have stopped walking. I can't hear what they are saying, but I can feel the stares.

"I have to run to a class, but he's in his office, just down there." She points to a door a few feet away before saying goodbye and turning to go quickly back up the stairs. Taking a deep breath, I raise my hand and knock on the door as I push it open.

When I walk in, I don't get a chance to take in anything other than the beautiful brunette perched on the edge of the huge glass desk. She's obviously not here to work out, based on the skin-tight pencil skirt she's wearing. The way she's sitting on the edge of the desk with her legs crossed has the material stretched precariously tight. Her shirt isn't faring much better, the open buttons showing a hint of the bra she's wearing. She makes me feel like I just crawled in here in my pajamas.

She turns to me as I stand in the doorway, unmoving. She's beautiful, but in a cold way. Her dark eyes are sharp and assessing, and everything about her screams sex. From her bright red lips to the sharp nails that are tapping on the desk. She makes no move to stand as she continues to stare.

Is this why he wanted me to text before I got here? So he could get the Jessica Rabbit lookalike out before I turned up? I'm aware I'm probably being overdramatic, but keeping my cool is damn hard. I've been here and done this before, and there is no chance I'm doing it again. I can feel my heartbeat accelerating in my chest, and my eyes narrow as I prepare to ask who she is, but she beats me to it.

"Can I help you?" Gah, even her voice is attractive, low and husky sounding.

I don't get a chance to answer before Keir walks into the office from what appears to be a bathroom on the other side of the room. He looks up to see me standing there and the smile that emerges on his face is enough to make me melt a little inside. That's not the smile of a man who just got caught doing something he shouldn't. His eyes crinkle at the sides and the dimples I've missed so much peep out for a second.

"Hey," he says, as he strides toward me. I take all of him in; his long legs encased in those ridiculously tight compression pants that show off every curve of each and every muscle in his legs. Unfortunately for me, he's once again added a pair of loose running shorts over the top. The tight tee covering his chest only serves to highlight the muscles there too. His silky, dark hair looks as if he's been running is hands through it all day. The urge to climb him like a tree is strong.

His smile never falters as he walks over to me. When he makes it to just a few feet in front of me, he reaches up and once again wraps his hand around my neck, dragging me forward to capture my lips with his. The move makes me forget that I was about to go to war with the other woman in the room.

Shifting my hands up the chest I was just admiring, I push them up further still, into the hair at the nape of his neck, and let my fingers play with the thick strands of slightly damp hair. His lips play with mine for a second before his tongue peeks out briefly to gently touch mine.

All too soon, he's moving his mouth from mine and I feel the loss somewhere below my belly. I'm lost in the lust-filled haze he just threw me into, so I miss what she says, but Jessica Rabbit must have spoken because Keir's eyes leave mine and fly to her. I notice they narrow slightly when he sees her there. She's moved to stand next to the desk now, but is making no attempt to leave.

"Morgen, what are you still doing here?" he asks, not moving his hand from my waist when I turn fully to face her.

"I had a few questions I forgot to ask, so I was waiting for you to come back," she says, biting on her lower lip. Her eyes are eating him up like he's a meal and she's starving.

"Can it wait? I have plans," Keir says, giving my waist a small squeeze. Her eyes flick over to me for a split second before they jump back to his.

"Of course, I'm sorry to interrupt." She reluctantly starts to collect her stuff. Once she's ready to leave, she stops in front of us.

"Sorry again, it was nice to meet you…" She trails off as she offers her hand for me to shake.

"Poppy, this is Morgen. Morgen, this is my girlfriend, Poppy." Keir looks at me apologetically, and I don't know if it's because he called me his girlfriend or if it's because she seems reluctant to leave us alone. I don't react to it outwardly, not wanting to give her the satisfaction, but internally, I'm terrified. One evening of making out after ten years apart does not make me his girlfriend.

After the world's briefest handshake, she finally leaves. Once the door shuts behind her, he spins me around and his mouth is back on mine, making me lose whatever thoughts were beginning to fester in my mind.

This time, his lips devour mine, his tongue demanding entry again. His arms band around me, dragging me against his body, and I feel every inch of him. With both of our hands now exploring each other, I drop my head to the side slightly, allowing him access to my neck. His stubbled jaw drives me crazy, and he makes his way from underneath my ear down to my shoulder. When my shirt gets in his way, he lets out a groan that I feel vibrate through my body, all the way to my clit. Moving to rest his forehead against mine, he stares deeply into my eyes. The mahogany depths search mine for something, I can only guess he finds what he's looking for because he gives me another panty-melting smile.

"Can we always say hello like this?"

Seventeen

Keir

Holding Poppy in my arms as she laughs is a dream come true and once again, I have to fight the urge to pinch myself to make sure it's real. Pecking her lips once more softly, I reluctantly let her go. Her smile is like a ray of light crashing down on me, warming me from the inside out.

Walking in here and seeing her standing there made my heart jump in my chest. Even finding Morgen still in here couldn't knock me from the high I'm on right now. I know she was bullshitting about having more questions for me. There was no need at all for the last-minute meeting she asked for today. She's been trying to get into my pants for the last year, ever since she took over as our supplement sales rep. She's yet to take no for an answer, but I'm hopeful that seeing Poppy here today will get her to stop. Calling her my girlfriend had been a slip of the tongue and for a second, I'd frozen in place, terrified that Poppy might run. So much for taking it slowly. I'm going to pretend it didn't happen, unless she brings it up herself.

"Let me just finish up here and we can go."

I move to my desk to shut everything down, but I'm finding it nearly impossible to drag my eyes away from Poppy. She moves around the space, looking at the pictures on the walls. There are poster-size pictures of me at all stages of my career, all caught mid-game. There's a few of my jerseys framed up there too. She stops in front of a picture of me playing in college.

It's a picture of me with my helmet off, hair looking crazy. I'm looking off camera into the stands with a huge smile on my face. She doesn't know it, but I'm looking at her as she walks toward me. It was the first game she came to, and she had surprised me by wearing my name on her back. I remember feeling like I could have played the other team single-handed, I was that pumped on adrenaline at seeing it on her. She also doesn't know that when my mom took that picture, she also took one of the moment she ran into my arms right there on the field. That picture is hidden away in my closet at home.

"You don't talk much about it," Poppy says, without looking at me.

"About what?"

"Your career. I know where you played, but what was it like?" She turns and walks toward me, stopping on the other side of the desk. "Was it everything you hoped it would be?"

I'm not sure how to answer this one. I'm still conflicted over my time playing pro. As much as I'd loved the game, I never liked all the bullshit that came with it. The photoshoots and sponsorship crap. The constant intrusion into every part of my life sucked too. Deciding now isn't the time to get into all this, I go with the easy answer.

"There's not much in life that can compare to pulling on that jersey and running out onto that field," I say with a genuine smile on my face. I don't add that being here, with her back in my life, comes pretty damn close to that feeling. I can tell that she wants to ask more questions, but something holds her back. If there is any chance it could be something that upsets her, I'm not going to push it. Yet another thing to be filed away for some other time.

Once I've showered and changed, and we're ready to leave, I grab a hold of Poppy's hand. There's no way I'm letting her walk through this place without letting every fucker in here know that she's off-limits. I'm already pissed that she didn't tell me she was here earlier. The thought of the guys looking at her in those shorts is enough to get my blood boiling.

As we pass the guys in the ring, I hope to God that we can somehow sneak past without them noticing us. I'm shit outta luck when I see them all stop and stare. Speeding up my steps, I pull Poppy out of there before they can start busting my balls. I've hardly ever so much as looked at a woman in the gym, let alone walked out holding one by the hand.

"Stop it, will you?" She giggles as we make it to the stairwell. The door slams shut behind us and being alone in a dark place with her is not an opportunity I'm about to pass up.

I push her body into the wall next to the door. Her gasp barely has time to form before my mouth covers hers. Lifting her by her ass, I urge her legs around my waist. I have no idea why I keep torturing myself this way. Feeling her hot pussy against me drives me fucking wild, and I grind her harder against me. My dick feels like it's about to burst through my pants. If I don't slow this down, she's going to make me come like a damn teenager. My poor balls are so confused, and it looks like another night of trying to control myself before I can go home and rub one out. Who am I kidding? More like, rub two or three out.

I'm saved from having to stop the kiss when the door at the top of the stairs opens. I feel Poppy freeze for a second before her legs fall from around my hips. She pushes me back slightly, and tries in vain to smooth out the wild mess my hands have made of her hair.

She's always beautiful but seeing her like this, cheeks flushed, and lips swollen and red, makes me want to beat on my chest like a caveman.

TJ appears through the doorway, doing a double take when he's sees us. The stupid grin on his face tells me he knows exactly what's gone on here.

"Sorry to interrupt you guys," he says smugly. The bastard is loving this. Moving down the stairs toward us, he gives Poppy a quick kiss on the cheek before punching me in the arm. "If you two aren't busy tonight, a few of us are meeting at Maggie's for a few beers. You should join us."

I had originally planned to take her back to my place, but it's obvious that my idea to take this thing between us slowly will never work if we're alone anywhere near a bed.

"That sounds fine with me," I say, looking at Poppy to gauge her reaction. She smiles and gives me a nod.

"Great, let me just go grab my shit and we'll drive over together," he says as he walks away, flashing me a satisfied grin when Poppy can't see it. He'll be lucky if he doesn't end up with my foot in his ass by the end of the night.

Eighteen

Poppy

This night is a disaster.

We arrived an hour ago to find a booth full of guys. After lots of introductions, where I notice Keir doesn't again introduce me as his girlfriend, I was surprised to find that his friends are really nice. Most of them are guys from his gym, but a few are friends he's had since school. I'd relaxed into the booth and listened as the good-natured ribbing flew back and forth between them all. Keir's hand placed gently on my thigh hadn't hurt at all either.

The night took a turn for the worse when a group of women joined us. When Keir introduced them, they'd given me fake smiles and promptly turned to sit as far away from me as possible. I then had to sit and listen to them regale stories of past nights out and all the *fun* they've all had.

After yet another story that's meant to remind me they had a place in his life, I've had enough. Excusing myself, I make my way into the bathroom. I lock the stall door and drop the toilet seat lid before sitting down. The door bangs open a few minutes later, and the Witches of Eastwick stand outside the stall door. I can't freaking escape them.

"Double denim? Really? He never brings anyone around and when he finally does, that's it?"

I can't tell which one speaks, but I couldn't care less which one it is. The derision in her tone makes my back stiffen. I'm not in the least bit surprised they're talking about me.

"I heard from Jana that he's an absolute beast in the sack," another of them says.

"Are you surprised? No one lives the life he has without picking up a ton of experience. Trust me," the third one throws in, sounding all-together too smug. I get the feeling she's talking from experience. I feel sick thinking about Keir with anyone else. I know that we've been apart, and I know he's done nothing wrong, but my insecurities missed the memo.

Leaning forward to pull my phone out from my back pocket, I type a message to Elliott. I've already been keeping her up to date as the night has dragged on.

Me: HELP

Me: I NEED RESCUING!

El: What's wrong?

Me: I'm stuck in a bad movie!!

El: Huh?

El: WTF Pop?? What's going on?

Me: Came into the bathroom to escape the Keir Harmon Groupie meeting and they've followed me in!

Me: They're talking about how good he is in bed. Stop me from going out there and pulling out her bad hair extensions!

The three dots bounce around for a minute before they disappear. I wait a few seconds, but they start up again before I can reply.

El: Front it out. Walk out with a smile on your face. Even if it kills you to do it.

Me: Will you bail me out if I need it?

El: Always

Taking a deep breath, I stand and pull the flush. The chatter outside stops and I'm not surprised to see them all looking at the door as I step out of the stall. The blonde is the only one that looks even a little embarrassed to be caught talking shit about me. The other two share a knowing smirk, so I know they planned this little ambush.

"Ladies." I give them a wide smile as I wash my hands, trying like hell to show they haven't affected me like they wanted to. They stay silent as I move toward the door, but their stares never waver. Once the door is open and I'm about to step outside, I turn back to them.

"Oh, by the way," I say, surprising them, "you're right. He really is a beast in bed."

Letting the door slam behind me, I quickly make my way back to the table. I don't know what expression is on my face but as soon as he sees me coming, Keir is on his feet.

"What's wrong?" He takes a hold of my upper arms as his eyes scan my body quickly. "What's going on?"

Swallowing down the lump of emotion his concern brings up, I force a smile. "Nothing, I'm just tired. I'm going to head out."

Letting go of my arms, he wraps one of his big hands around mine and moves us both to the table. Stopping to pick up his keys, he starts saying goodbye to the guys seated there.

"No, you stay. I'll get a cab," I say, trying unsuccessfully to remove my hand from his.

"Not happening, baby girl," he says, without letting me go. "TJ, you good to get a ride home?"

His brother nods, as he glances my way. I'm so irrationally fucking mad at Keir, but I try to hide it in front of his friends, not wanting to cause a scene. Keeping the fake smile on my face, I wait for Keir to say his goodbyes. I avoid looking at anyone, but when TJ asks me if I'm ok, I'm scared I might crack. I can feel tears burning the back of my nose as I nod.

Keir manages to get us outside without being stopped by anyone. All night, there have been crowds of people wanting a bit of him. It's not until we're in the truck that he speaks again.

"What happened in there?"

If there was one thing I learned from the way our relationship ended last time, it's that honest communication is vital.

"Your fan club ambushed me in the bathroom." I look at him as I speak, proud of myself for not breaking down in tears. He's concentrating on the road, but his brow furrows as he hears my words.

"Who?"

"The three groupies that were hanging around. They tried to act like they didn't know I was in there, but it was obvious they knew."

"What the fuck?" His hands tighten on the wheel and a part of me wants to comfort him, tell him not to get worked up. But the other part of me is pissed. Pissed at those girls for being bitchy. Pissed at myself for letting them get under my skin. Pissed at Keir for having a life without me.

"Tell me what they said, Poppy," he grits out. I don't know why he's angry. It was me who had to hear them.

"Just drop it, Keir," I bite out, wanting this discussion finished. "Just take me home."

"Tell me."

"I said, take me home."

"Just fucking tell me!" he shouts as he slams his hand down on the steering wheel, and something inside me snaps.

"They couldn't wait to talk about how good you are in bed, ok!" I yell. "I had to sit in there and listen to that shit, so don't fucking shout at me!"

My chest is heaving when I'm done, and I just want out of here. I want away from it all. This is why I've kept myself closed off. Feeling like this is fucking horrible. The memories of all the girls in college that tried to come between us. The fights over how they would throw themselves at him. Each and every one of those old feelings is coming back, and I can't stand it.

Keir doesn't say a word, his jaw clamped shut so tightly I can see the tendons straining in his neck. He yanks the truck around and I see we've made it to my house. We lurch to a stop and before I can do anything, he's got his belt undone and he's marching around to my side of the truck. There's no way I'm staying in here, the anger racing through me. Pushing the door open, I jump down to the ground but I don't get far before his large body is blocking my way. He pushes me back against the truck and lowers his face to mine.

"Listen to me." His voice is low and hard, and I'm ashamed to admit that I feel it *everywhere.* "I have not now, nor have I ever, touched any of them."

His words should soothe me, but I don't think anything could calm me right now. He won't understand. It doesn't matter if he touched her. It doesn't matter if she's lying. The problem won't go away because the problem is me; I don't know how to let my insecurities go. I stare into his eyes that are scanning mine, looking for something that I don't think he'll find.

I can't take any more of the feelings that are crashing over me, so I do the only thing I know that will make me forget.

I kiss him.

I kiss him until my lungs are filled with his air.

I kiss him until the confusion is chased away, and all I can think of is him and the fire he lights inside of me.

Nineteen

Keir

When her lips slam down onto mine, I can feel her bare desperation seeping through. When she groans into my mouth, I use it to my advantage and push my tongue even further into hers. Letting my hands travel down from her waist, I cup her ass and bring her legs up and around my waist. Our tongues continue to dual as her hands touch any part of me they can reach. Moving us toward the house, I don't let her down as I walk up the porch steps. The feeling of her lightly bouncing against my rock-solid length is almost enough to have me come in my pants. The way she's licking my neck does little to help how on edge I'm feeling.

"Keys, Pop." She gasps as I growl the words against her ear.

"Back pocket," she whispers back breathlessly.

Opening the door, I quickly get us inside before slamming it closed again. I wanted to take my time with her the first time I had her again, but that's not going to happen. I'm too amped, my blood is on fire. After another minute of making out against the door, I let her slide down my body. Each part of her that touches me sets off fireworks against my skin. Grabbing her by the hand, I demand to know where her room is, practically dragging her. Once we're inside, I spin her to face me.

"Tell me this is ok." I don't ask, I practically beg her. Her huge eyes look into mine, clear and sure.

"More than ok," and that's all I needed to hear.

We move together, meeting in a clash of hands and lips. She pushes my jacket off my shoulders as I rip the snap buttons on her shirt open, getting my first look at her fantastic tits. Unable to stop myself, I drop my head and suck a lace-covered nipple into my mouth. Wrapping my hands around her waist, I yank her closer, grinding my dick into her belly as she jams her fingers into my hair and pulls, hard. The slight pain spurs me on even more as I switch to her other nipple; this time, I yank down on the lace that's in my way. Feeling the stiff peak hit the roof of my mouth, I let out a groan of my own.

"Please let me feel you," Poppy says as she starts to yank on my t-shirt.

Hating to let her out of my reach, but longing to feel her skin on mine, I move back just far enough to pull it over my head, throwing it blindly somewhere in the room. I don't get to put my mouth back on her before she has hers on my skin, just below my ear. Her hot breath causes my skin to prickle with goose bumps, but it's her whimpering "Please" against my neck that snaps the thin thread of control I was clinging to.

Her hands find my belt as I lift her by the back of her knees and tip her backwards onto the bed. Taking her right leg in my hands, I gently remove her shoe before placing a kiss on her ankle. Moving to her other leg, I do the same, never letting my gaze drop from hers. I keep going, slowly kissing my way up. Once I get to the junction of her thighs, I place a kiss just above the waistband of her shorts as I slowly open the button and lower her fly, still watching her face.

I can't believe I'm here, in this moment. Here, with the only woman I've ever loved. I'm afraid that if I look away from her, all of this will disappear, and I'll be at home, alone. That's how my dreams usually go. Once I have her shorts down and removed, I'm suddenly overwhelmed. Letting my head drop down, I rest it on her stomach. Feeling her shift enough to reach me, her fingers sift through my hair.

"Keir…" she starts, but trails off when I lift my head to look at her again. Her hand moves to cup my cheek and it's an automatic response for me to turn into the touch. She could tell me to get up and get dressed right now, and that touch would be enough for me. I'm praying like fuck she doesn't because my dick might fall off if I deny it what it wants one more time. But knowing she's here in this moment with me fills me with some emotion I can't even describe.

"Come here."

Without resisting, I lift myself off the bed and remove my jeans. Her eyes never leave me as I move back toward her. She shifts her legs restlessly as I crawl to her, finally dropping them to the side, allowing me space to settle between her thighs. Finding her lips once again, I let her taste take over my senses. Let it calm my raging need. There are no words between us, just low murmurs. Each touch between us is a silent affirmation.

Letting my hands trace over the curves I once knew better than anything, it's not long before Poppy is writhing with need beneath me. Her breath has turned choppy and her heart hammers out her need against my chest as mine echoes it right back.

Sliding my hand up her thigh, I stop teasing her and let my fingers slip beneath the scrap of silk that's still covering her. When I feel how wet she is, my resolve is gone, and I quickly peel the underwear off her. Once they're gone, I can't help but stare at her, spread out before me. Wild hair fans over the white sheets, her impeccable tits pushed up by the bra that's sitting low where I pulled it down earlier. Legs spread, showing a glimpse of her wet center. She's a fucking vision. She gasps as I lean down and throw her legs over my shoulders.

"What are you...oh my God."

Her words slide into a moan as I lick my way up to her clit. Taking a peek up at her, I see her head is thrown back, hands pulling at her nipples. So I do it again, licking my way up and down, before I tease her entrance with my tongue.

"You taste so fucking sweet." It's like an explosion across my tongue. Fucking hell, I need to be inside her before I lose my shit. After showing just her clit some attention, I switch it up and kiss my way up and down her slit. Bringing her legs together, I press them up toward her chest, my hands spanning the back of her thighs.

"Fuck," I rumble against the skin on the back of her thighs, the vibrations making her twist the sheets in a fierce hold, before kissing my way back down.

I can't wait any longer. She needs to come right the fuck now. Sucking her clit into my mouth once more, I sink two fingers into her entrance, plunging them inside. Her back arches off the bed as her pussy starts to spasm, clenching around my fingers.

"Keir!" she shrieks, this time as she comes loudly, the moans making my balls tighten in anticipation.

Letting both legs go, they fall limply to the bed, just wide enough for me to fit between. Leaning over her on one arm, I gently kiss her lips. Her eyes open and she gives me a stunning smile. Taking a hold of myself in one hand, I tease her with the head of my dick, running it up and down her slit.

"You're so fucking wet." Not breaking eye contact, I gently slide inside of her.

"Oh fuck."

The words escape on a hiss. The moment I'm all the way in, everything else falls by the wayside. There are no thoughts, other than her and me. The feelings are almost too intense. The way her eyes never waver from mine steals my breath. There's no guard up now. It's just us and our feelings, stripped bare.

When she lifts her hips and slowly begins to move, my instincts kick in. The rhythm comes natural for us, our movements always in sync. Her pull, my push. It's like no time stands between us. The urge to see our connection drives me to lean back on my knees, I keep my hands on Poppy's waist, pulling her body into mine. The sight of her taking me like this is mesmerizing. When I feel her pussy start to spasm for the second time, I lose control once again. My movements turn wild, desperate to join her in tipping over the edge. When I come, the euphoria washes over me, leaving me feeling completely out of control for a few seconds.

As I come down, I barely manage to keep my weight off Poppy. My breathing feeling like it's never going to go back to normal, I've never felt more vulnerable in my life, like I've just laid myself bare for her to do whatever the fuck she wants with me.

Once I'm feeling more in control, I lift myself up. Poppy's hand flies up to stop me from moving too far.

"Stay," she says, giving me the most beautiful smile, letting me know without words that, for right now, things are ok.

Poppy

Parking my car outside of Deja Brew, I step out into the morning sunshine and let the rays warm my face. This is the most content I've felt for as long as I can remember. Who would have thought that the one thing I was most scared of would be the one to fill all of the gaps in my heart. Letting those thoughts show in the smile I'm wearing, I push the door to the coffee shop open. I see Elliott seated at a table in the back, and I weave my way through to her.

"Oh my God," she gasps when she sees me, making me stop before I pull the empty chair out.

"What?" I ask, looking around me to see what she's shocked about.

"You got laid!"

Feeling the heat explode onto my face, I do the only thing I can do. I stand and gape at her for a beat.

“Elliott Walker! What the hell is wrong with you?” I grit out. I’ve no idea why I’m surprised at her behavior. She has zero filter.

“Don't change the subject. You got laid, and I haven’t been told any of the details,” she whisper-yells right back at me. I’m so glad I have my back to the rest of the packed shop, I’m so freaking embarrassed.

“Since when do I tell you when I get laid.” I don't miss the happy dance she does in her seat at my admission that I have, in fact, gotten laid.

“Because this time, it’s Keir. No one else mattered.” She’s practically giddy. Refraining from rolling my eyes at her, I give in, just a little.

“Fine.” I have to fight my grin. “What do you want to know?”

“Everything.” She sighs.

Of course she does.

An hour and two coffees later, I’ve told her all about the fight that ended up in my bed. I don't give her details. Those are between Keir and I.

I don’t tell her how his touch lit my body on fire. Or that when he tucked me in next to him afterward, I felt the safest I’d ever been in years. How he’d stayed the night and spend most of it inside me. I also don't tell her that I’d had to bite back the urge to tell him I loved him. That was what scared me more than anything. The urge to just slip back into being with him. Old habits really do die hard.

While I am certain I'm doing the right thing, giving him a second chance, I have to take my time. As easy as it would be to shout from the rooftops that I'm in love, I know how hard the fall can be. I don't think any amount of running would save me if things were to go wrong again. No, I'm doing this thing the right way. Keir says that as long as I'm with him, he'll go as slowly as I need. So, no, I don't tell her everything.

"I'm happy for you, Pop. You deserve to be happy." Elliott reaches out and grabs my hand. Giving it a small squeeze, she goes on, "And I'll feed him his balls if he hurts you again," making us both laugh.

"So, enough about me. How are you? The girls ok?" Elliott immediately finds her coffee cup very interesting.

Oh no, if she thinks taking a drink of her coffee will distract from the grimace that just passed over her face, she's crazy. Taking the bull by the horns, I decide it's time she start telling me what the hell is going on with her.

"Did I do something?" I ask her.

"What? Why on earth would you think that?" Her back straightens in her chair. It's a low blow for me to play on her emotions like this, but watching my very best friend fade away more and more, each time I see her, is killing me.

"I'm supposed to be your best friend, yet you're obviously going through some stuff and you won't tell me what it is. I can only assume it's because of me." I feel like a bitch when I see tears fill her eyes. "If you don't want to tell me, that's one thing, but if you feel like you can't, that's a whole other story. You should know I'm always here for you."

She leans over to grab both of my hands, not bothering to wipe away the tear that leaks out.

"My gosh, Pop! I would never...I mean, I didn't think…I don't think—" Stopping herself from rambling on, she takes a deep breath and lets it out before looking at me again, as if gathering the courage to speak. "Pete's cheating on me."

My eyes widen and my breath catches in my throat. Those words are the last I ever expected her to hear her say.

After letting Elliott cry on my shoulder, I'm exhausted. As much as I begged her to bring the girls to stay with me, she would not back down. Her douchebag husband admitted he's been seeing someone else for the last year, but swears it's over. Seeing her so torn between following her instinct to leave or staying for the sake of the girls, has me so angry. He's obviously been wearing her down. I just wish she would have come and spoken to me sooner.

Once she's left to collect the girls from kindergarten, I pull out my laptop to get some work done. I get lost in a new job and before I know it, two hours have passed. I'm just about to pack up and head home when I feel a presence at my back. Before I can turn around, I feel warm lips touch my neck, just below my ear. My face splits into a huge grin. I don't need to turn around to know who it is.

"Hey baby." The vibrations of the words spoken directly on my skin make me shiver as goose bumps race up and down my arms.

"Hey," I reply, as he takes the seat Elliott vacated earlier. "What are you doing here?"

"Well, you said you were meeting Elliott here this morning, and since you haven't answered any of my texts, I took a chance and…" He trails off, a sheepish look on his face. "I just realized how stalkerish that sounds."

I try to keep the stern look on my face, I really do, but he's so damn cute, I can't help but laugh at him. Especially when he blushes ever so slightly. When he lifts his ball cap from his head, his dark hair is a mess, and I itch to reach out and push my fingers through it. He's so handsome it hurts to look at him sometimes. The dark stubble on his jaw makes me think of how it felt when he feasted on me like a starving man last night. Squirming in my seat, I quickly look away, hoping he can't read my thoughts. I clear my throat and start to speak, but the words come out shaky.

"I'm sorry, I forgot I left my phone on silent. El is going through some stuff, and I wanted her to have all my attention for a minute."

He immediately looks concerned and I know it's genuine. One of the things I fell in love with when I first met him was his compassion. If he could do something to fix someone's problems, he would do it in a heartbeat. It's no surprise when he immediately asks if he can do anything to help her.

“I think she just needs support.” I debate on whether or not to tell him what’s going on. We’ve pretty much managed to avoid all talk of the past, specifically the mistake he made. I’m not sure how this reminder will go down.

Fuck it.

“Her husband has been cheating on her.”

I rip the band-aid off. If we can’t get through a conversation about someone else’s infidelity, then we have no chance of making it all.

I don’t miss the flinch. Shifting uncomfortably on his seat, he doesn't immediately say anything. After almost a minute of silence, he finally speaks.

“Are they getting a divorce?”

He looks at me, and all I see in his eyes is a mix of regret and guilt. The fact that he recognizes that his actions ten years prior still have ramifications today should make me feel better, but in all honesty, talking about it all morning has stirred up a boatload of horrible memories for me.

“I wish they would, but I get the feeling he’s trying to guilt her into staying for the girls.” I sigh.

We sit in a silence that’s so thick with unsaid words that I almost regret telling him.

“I, uh, need to get home to see to Frank. Was there something you needed me for? Or was the stalking just for fun?”

I try for levity, but it falls flat. Probably because my heart isn't in it. It's not my fault that things turned awkward, but I need to get out of here. As I pack away my laptop and notebooks, I feel Keir's stare on me. He doesn't say anything, just follows behind me, as I make my way outside.

"I just wanted to see if you had plans for the long weekend?" I forgot that I'd even asked him a question.

"I know you probably already made plans, but if not, I was thinking of heading over to the cabin at Tybee?"

"You guys still have that place?"

"Dad would never give that place up. Anyway, I know you said to go slow, but I'm going to be there, and I didn't want to be without you for the whole weekend. I've not spent much time with them lately."

Can I do this? My head says that it's a bad idea, that I should put on the brakes a little. My heart, however, says a whole weekend without him feels like a terrible idea.

"Bring Frank, I'm sure he'll love the beach."

The awkwardness from earlier lifts slightly as Keir steps closer to me, giving me a shy smile. He drops his head and kisses me sweetly on my lips. Once, twice, before dipping his tongue inside for the smallest of tastes. He knows I'm weak when his mouth is on mine. Before I can complain that he's a tease, I find myself saying yes.

That damn man and his magical kisses.

Poppy

I can't believe I let him talk me into this.

Damn him and his kisses that leave me stupid.

Three days in a cabin with the entire Harmon family?

Heaven help me.

Getting myself situated in the cab of the stupidly large truck, I pull out my sunglasses and my iPad, hoping that Keir takes the hint and leaves me alone. I let my eyes wander to the scenery passing quickly by. Savannah in the summer is easily the most beautiful place I've ever lived. The lush trees flying by are almost hypnotic, but it's impossible to stop my mind wandering. I feel like I'm stuck halfway between memories of what we used to be, and the reality of what we're trying to become now.

Especially this trip.

I can't forget the times we would drive over and spend the weekends with his family. I loved being with them and for the year we were together, his mom, Diana, was more of a mother to me than anyone ever had been before, and Ted was the father figure that I didn't realize had been missing from my life. In twelve short months, they took me in and accepted me. My insecurities and lack of understanding about family dynamics were not an issue for this crazy, loveable bunch. Even when his dad had been diagnosed with cancer a few months after we met, they'd been a unit. A solid group that worked together to get him through it.

The last ten years without them has been difficult. I hadn't just lost a boyfriend, I'd lost a family. I couldn't bear to keep in touch with them because the thought of bumping into Keir or listening to Diana talk about what he was doing was just too much.

We've only been on the road a few minutes when Keir's voice breaks the not so comfortable silence.

"I meant to apologize for the way I reacted at the coffee shop."

That voice. The deep rumble that I feel ripple all the way through me anytime he speaks. It always did have that effect on me. It didn't matter if he was whispering sweet nothings in my ear or quoting mind-numbing football stats, his voice always did it for me.

"We have so much that we still need to talk about, but hearing you talk about Pete and what he did? I just didn't know how to react. I mean, how can I call him a prick when I was no better than him once?"

I'm shocked to hear he thinks of himself that way. I shift in my seat to face him before speaking.

"Keir, you made a mistake. Did I hate you for it? Yeah. For a while, I really did." I hate seeing the way his jaw tightens at my words, but I keep going. "I'm choosing to believe that you learned from that mistake. I have to trust that you won't do it again, otherwise what's the point of this?" I ask, waving my hand back and forth in the space between us.

I mean it. Will I have doubts sometimes? I'm sure I will, but I can't let myself get stuck back there. He moves to grab my hand and squeezes it gently before bringing it to his mouth. I want to go and sit as close to him as possible, but Frank has decided to sleep across the bench seat, leaving me pretty much stuck against the door.

"I swear, you have nothing to ever worry about with that, Pop. I know what losing you feels like, and I'm never going back there."

His declaration clears the air in the cab a little and we quickly fall into a more comfortable silence. It's not until we get closer to the cabin that I start to panic slightly. I'm scared. Scared that Diana hates me now for not responding to her many attempts to contact me over the years. That they somehow blame me. That deep-seated fear that I somehow pushed Keir into cheating; the feeling they believe that it was my fault is stubborn as fuck and won't go away.

I feel his hand gently land on mine where I have it absently stroking Frank's head, giving me another small squeeze. “I can take you back. I’m being insensitive throwing you in with my family like this.”

I’m not surprised he can read my mood so easily; he always could, after all. Swinging my head around to face him, I let my gaze linger on him a while. Wild hair that looks like it’s a month or two past due for a cut, that ridiculous jawline that’s still dusted with a few days’ worth of stubble. He’s wearing the softest, worn gray shirt, and I couldn't help but notice his ass in those worn jeans when he helped get Frank and my bags into the car earlier. His eyes, covered with his Aviators, stop me from seeing the feelings hidden in his eyes. I always loved his eyes, they used to tell me more than his words ever did. Maybe that why I’m feeling disjointed? Because I’m missing his eyes. They were one of the things I missed most over the years, the molten brown depths that used to drown me.

“It’s fine. I’ll be fine. I just don’t know how to be around your family, that’s all.”

“Just be you, Pop. You did nothing wrong, and my family knows that.”

I can’t help but notice how his jaw ticks with that small mention of the past. We really need to learn to be able to talk about it freely. We have so many good memories, it feels wrong to dismiss them all because we’re both scared to go back there.

“Your mother tried to stay in touch, you know.”

Keir doesn’t look the least bit shocked at this news. “Were you really surprised? She loved you more than she loved me.” Our small laughs bounce around the cab.

"I'll never forget how disappointed she was in me…they all were." His voice is gruff, barely even audible over the rumble of the engine and Frank's heavy breaths floating up from the seat between us. My heart feels heavy in my chest for him. No matter what he did to me, I hate the thought of Keir and his family not being on good terms.

"You told them?" I have no idea why this surprises me. The Harmon family does not keep secrets. They are the family that actually faces up to their mistakes. They tackle their problems as a team. I remember how they would all be involved with Teddy's treatments. How they would have meetings to discuss who would be at doctor's appointments, or helping out with whatever it was that Diana needed from them. Growing up with no real family, I had quickly fallen in love with their way of supporting one another, the way they offered unconditional love, no matter the circumstances.

"Yeah, and trust me when I say they practically cheered your ass for leaving me." There's no humor in his words and I know the truth behind them. As much as Di and Teddy love their boys, they wouldn't have condoned what Keir did. They were always hugely proud of his achievements, but to them staying humble was non-negotiable. I know he would have gotten a huge telling off from his mother.

"Don't judge me for this, but I checked up on them from time to time. TJ has his profile open on Facebook and I'd go take a look sometimes. I wanted to know how your dad's health was."

I'm blushing so hard at that admission. I don't want to see Keir's reaction to it, so I drop my eyes to Frank sleeping on the bench seat, and start playing with his soft fur. I can see Keir shift in his seat before he clears his throat and asks me the question I knew was coming next.

"So, uh, you could see all of TJ's posts, huh?"

Doing my best to keep my face blank, I reply with a deadpanned, "Yep," popping the P for extra effect. "You guys sure had some...interesting vacations."

Every year, Keir, TJ, and some their friends would go somewhere exotic for a few days. Seeing pictures of the man I never stopped loving draped in bikini-clad women was hellish, but like the masochist I obviously am, I couldn't stop myself looking. Repeatedly.

"I wouldn't trust everything you see on social media, Pop."

"Could have used that advice yourself ten years ago, Score."

We both wince at the bite of words and the nickname I have never used. A part of me wishes I could take them back. I have no idea where the attitude came from. Embarrassment heats my cheeks.

"Don't even think of apologizing." He can still read me like a book. "You're right, and I learned that lesson the hard way."

There isn't a lot that can be said after that, so the next hour of the journey passes in relative silence.

"Do we need to stop soon to let Frank out?"

I don't lift my head as I tell him the dog will be fine for a while yet. When we stop at a set of lights, I feel him reach over and turn my head away from where I've been concentrating on work emails.

Gently directing my gaze to meet his, he speaks quietly. "I know I sprung this weekend on you, but I genuinely want you to have a good time. I know my family has missed you, and I couldn't stand the thought of not seeing you."

His eyes trail over my face and I once again have to remind myself to breathe.

"I know we still have things to talk about. I think it's pretty obvious we need to clear the air."

I'm about to butt in and tell him he's wrong, that we're fine without bringing the past up. I don't want to go there. I'm happy to move forward without ever bringing that time up, but I know that's not healthy. Before I can say anything, he continues. "Let's make a deal. How about we stick a pin in it? I want to go and enjoy a few days at the beach with my family. I want to let my mother fuss all over me. I wanna eat whatever amazing food my dad is going to grill, and I wanna play some ball on the beach with TJ. I could even be convinced to play a few rounds of catch with Frank if he can be bothered to get his lazy ass up."

I can just see Frank roll his eyes at Keir without actually lifting his head, his expression clearly saying there is not much chance of *that* happening. The tension slowly seeps out from between us, and we sit in the stifling cab, just looking at each other. I don't know what he's seeing when he looks at me, but all I see from him is sincerity.

"Above any of that, what I really want? Is to catch up with my friend. You were my best friend as much as you were my girlfriend and I've missed you." His wry smile is the final nail of the coffin housing any potential doubts; for now, at least. I don't know what the future holds for us, but I want nothing more than to try and make this work.

Giving him a bright smile, I say, "Ted is in charge of the grill? Well, you should have led with that and I would have been in a better mood as soon as you picked me up."

With an eye roll, Keir shifts back into his seat and starts moving once the light switches to green.

It's not long before I see the signs telling us we're close to the cabin. Packing away the notebook I was using, I feel his hand stop my leg from its nonstop bouncing.

"Stop," he admonishes gently.

"Are you sure your parents are ok with me being here?"

Frank gave up on the cramped seats up here in the cab at our last rest stop, and is now stretched out full body on the blankets Keir laid out in the bed of the truck for him. There isn't anything between me and him now, so I can sit with my leg hitched up on the seat, turned toward Keir. It's because I'm sitting facing him fully that I don't miss his head drop slightly as he winces, raising a hand to scratch the back of his neck as he pulls into the driveway. *Oh fuck.* That's a classic guy move when they've done something wrong and don't know how to admit it.

I'm going to kill him.

Kill him *dead.*

Then I'm going to revive him, so I can kill him again.

"You didn't. Tell me you didn't." It's a miracle my back teeth haven't smashed to pieces from being ground together so tightly.

"Well, see...the thing is…there wasn't much time and…I didn't exactly plan, and…"

His ramble is cut off by a loud shriek from outside the truck that is now stopped outside the Harmons' cabin. Closing my eyes slowly, I bite back to urge to poke him in the eye.

"See? Told you she'd be happy to see you." He looks all too smug as he tries to hide his smile. Before I can come up with a retort, my door is flung open and my arms are full of Keir's mom. She wraps herself around me as best she can while I'm still seated. My own eyes are also wet with tears as she cries happy tears into my shoulder.

Twenty-Two

Keir

Seeing the sheer joy on my mother's face soothes the fear I had that this might have been a bad idea. Poppy hasn't even made it out of the truck, but my mom has still managed to fold her into a hug. I can hear them both sniffing through tears. They'd had such a close relationship before, and I don't think my mom ever got over the disappointment I caused her.

Moving around the truck, I open the tailgate so Frank can jump down, and he immediately runs around the yard. I'm pretty sure that's the first time I've ever seen his lazy ass move that fast.

By the time I've carried our bags to the porch, my dad has appeared at the front door.

"Well shit, son." He laughs softly as he sees who my mum is hugging. "This is one hell of a surprise."

"I know. I'm still shocked she's giving me the time of day, let alone a second chance."

Not taking his eyes off the two women, he speaks again. 'She's a rare one, son. The ones that have a beautiful heart."

He's right, of course.

"You know what it feels like to lose it, Keir. Don't make the same mistake this time." There's no judgment in his words. Just honesty.

"Never, Dad."

Giving me a clap on the back, he makes his way down the wooden steps where he gently takes Poppy from my mother and wraps her in his arms. The sound of her crying causes the now familiar lump in my throat to spring up once again.

No, there's no way I'll ever risk losing this again.

A few hours later, I'm standing at the water's edge, the cool water splashing against my shins. The day has gone much better than I could ever have hoped. Having Poppy here feels so fucking right. It's like she's never been away.

I feel her as she steps up behind me, before she touches me. The air always changes when she's near. That split second before her skin touches mine, I can sense her. She rests her head against the middle of my back and snakes her arms around me, linking her hands together.

When she's here like this, I can breathe easier. Its inexplicable, but true. It's also one of the real reasons I brought her here. When we're together, I know she's *here.* It's the time that we're apart that causes that tiny part of her that wants to run to flare to life. She tells me with words that she wants this, but I'm terrified that she might forget the undeniable connection between us if we're apart for too long.

"She finally let you go then?"

My mother has not let Poppy out of her sight since she stepped out of the truck earlier. I feel the laugh she lets out as a rush of hot air against my bare skin and it causes my cock to swell. This woman will be the death of me. We've not spent the night together since that one night. I've been trying hard to give her some of that space she asked for, but I'm not sure how much longer I can go before I crack.

"She's just excited."

"And so are you?"

"Of course, thank you for inviting me."

I have to shift her around so she's in front of me, I can't take any more of her hot breath on me. She's wearing those damn denim shorts again, and she's thrown on one of my old hoodies. Wrapping my arms around her waist, I lift her gently, so I can kiss her.

"Never thank me for wanting to spend time with you," I say, without taking my mouth off hers.

"I know things have been a little up and down with us, but I want you to know, I really am happy you're back in my life, Keir."

Her words fill some of the tiny cracks inside me. Kissing her once more, I move us so we're sitting on the warm sand. The sun is close to setting and we spend a minute, just enjoying the view. There's something about the calm of this moment, something that is just so *right*. I know I'm where I'm supposed to be, with the one person that was made for me. Poppy is my world and I know in this moment, she'll be my person forever. I'll never stop working to prove to her that what we have, and everything that we will have in the future, means everything to me.

I live everyday with regrets over the past, but there is tiny part of me that wonders where we would have ended up if I hadn't fucked up. I'm certain she would have hated that life. She would have tried, my Poppy is not a quitter, but she would have been miserable. Would she have resented me? The thought of us drifting apart kills me.

"I came back for you." My words float out, and a small part of me hopes she doesn't hear them, that they get swept out to sea like the sand at our feet. I know that isn't the case when she shifts to look at me.

"What do you mean?"

"Back then. When I woke up that morning to find you'd gone, I knew I should let you go, but as hard as I tried, I couldn't fight the urge to go and get you. To get on my knees and beg you to forgive me."

Remembering how hard those times were causes a physical pain in my chest.

"We were stuck on the road for almost ten days. I've never played such shitty games in my life."

She doesn't laugh when I do, probably because there's no real humor in my words.

"As soon as we had some days off, I came back to Savannah for you."

As I get lost in the memories, she moves to straddle my lap. Her head rests on my shoulder, her forehead against the skin of my neck. I wonder, does she realize she does that every time she can?

"I was on my way to your place when I saw you. Sitting outside Addy's in your car. You looked so broken. The urge to go to you, to fix my mistake, was so fierce. But at the same time, I knew it wouldn't matter what I said or did. I'd never been good enough for you. I'd never be there, I wouldn't have been able to put you first. The team and that life would have come first, and every disappointment would have made you hate me more and more. It was inevitable. Even if, by some miracle, I could convince you to forgive me, it would have been selfish of me to keep you."

I feel the first tear hit my skin and I squeeze her closer to me. We stay there as the sun sets in the distance, as the blues and reds turn to inky black lit up by bright stars. After a long silence, her hoarse voice slices through the night.

"We're like the night sky."

“Yeah?”

“Yeah. You have to appreciate the dark, because without it, you wouldn’t see the stars.”

Just when I think I can’t fall for her any more than I already have, she goes and proves me so fucking wrong.

By the time we get back to the cabin, the sun is close to rising again, and we have sand in some very interesting places.

Twenty-three

Poppy

I'm being lazy in the afternoon sun, book in hand, when I feel a shadow move over me. Lifting my sunglasses, I see Ted lowering himself into the lounger next to mine. I can't help the grin that slides into place. I've exhausted my face muscles with how much I've been grinning the last few days.

"Hey," he says, returning my grin. He looks so healthy, it's amazing to see. Although he'd been in remission the last time I'd seen him, the treatments had left him frail. Keir and TJ both get their height and bulky build from their dad, so to see the usually strong man weakened had been heartbreaking.

"We are so glad you're here," he says, giving my arm a light squeeze. Placing my hand on top of his, I squeeze him back affectionately.

"I'm happy to be here. I missed you guys."

There had been a lot of tears shed when I'd tried to explain why I'd stayed away. Di told me repeatedly that she understood and told me in no uncertain terms that she was just happy to have me back. When I hear Ted let out a long sigh from next to me, I know he's out here with something to say. He never takes his eyes off where Keir and TJ are throwing a football back and forth, Frank trying to play piggy in the middle.

"He wasn't himself for a long while, you know, after you left."

I want to stop him and tell him that we're moving on from that, but for some reason, I stay quiet. I know Keir kind of went off the rails for a while—everyone that picked up a newspaper during that time knew he had a reputation. Not the good kind either.

"Sure, he played football. He had his wild ways and his fair share of trouble, but I mean, something deep in him changed. A part of him shut down."

My heart hurts for them all. For Keir, and for his family, who had to watch him withdraw into himself in front of their eyes.

Still, I don't speak. I blamed myself plenty over the years, second-guessed how I acted, how I might have pushed Kier away. It took a long time for me to move past those feelings and it's now rare that they pop into my head. I refuse to feel guilt for his actions. He's already told me his regrets and showered me with apologies.

I hear the guys let out a loud laugh as Frank somehow gets ahold of their ball and takes off for the beach that's just a few yards away. My eyes are like magnets, stuck on watching his toned body flex and roll as he ends up on the ground wrestling with the dog.

"TJ would drag him to so many different things, just to stop him being alone"—he laughs quietly—"but you could see his heart was never in it."

"I…" I attempt to speak but he cuts me off.

"If you're not all in, please don't let him think you are."

His words stun me. They also piss me off.

"Do you really think I would be here, with all of you, if I wasn't sure." I rip my glasses off so he can see my reaction to his words. "I'm not a kid anymore and I don't play games, Ted!" I exclaim. His words have my eyes filling with hot tears.

"Still the same little firecracker then?' He laughs at me, and I want to be offended, but there is no malice in his words. He just wants his son to be happy. "I know he was the one that made the mistake. I also know that you had every right to leave him. We have never judged you harshly for that, I swear. I also don't, for one minute, think you're playing games, Pop. I'm just terrified of that fear I see in your eyes. It's like you're waiting for the other shoe to drop."

Swinging his legs off the sun-lounger, he takes both my hand in his. My heart is galloping in my chest, the blood rushing in my ears. Is he right?

Fuck. I have been feeling like this is too good to be true.

Can it be this easy? Can we get it right this time?

"Seeing you two together is a dream come true for us. I promise you that. I'm just looking out for both of you."

I don't look him in the eye as I admit the one thing I've been denying, even to myself.

"What if it goes wrong again? I don't think I could survive it again." Tears fall freely now, scalding my skin as they fall.

"Poppy, I have every faith that you two will get it right this time. But it's *you* that has to have faith, not me," he whispers into my hair, his arms now around my shoulder.

Hours later, I'm tucked into Keir's side as he gently rocks us back and forth on the porch swing. I've been distracted all afternoon, Ted's words stuck on a loop in my mind. Not even the beautiful fireworks that have been lighting the night sky could distract me. The last few colorful splashes have faded away, and the feel of his fingers tracing patterns on my arm is about to send me to sleep.

Shifting off the swing, he reaches out a hand and helps me to stand. Keeping my hand in his, he gently pulls me through the silent house. When we reach his bedroom door, he pauses, silently asking if this is ok. I've been staying in the guest room, not wanting his parents to freak out. We've done nothing more than fool around a little since the first night he made love to me, but now I'm ready to feel that connection with him again. Ready to be loved by him. Ready to let him banish all the confusing thoughts swirling inside me.

The sound of the door lock sliding into place is the only noise to break the silence. Moving us to the bed, he lays me down gently before lying down next to me. Our lips gravitate to one another; it's instinctual. The kiss starts out soft and lazy, a sultry sweep of his soft lips on mine, but that frisson of need is ever-present.

"You're so fucking beautiful," he murmurs, just before he nips my bottom lip.

I tilt my head back to allow him to continue trailing hot kisses down my neck, and he doesn't disappoint. Open mouthed kisses leave me a heated mess. By the time he removes my shirt, kissing every exposed inch as he goes, I'm on the verge of detonating.

"I don't think I'll ever get enough of you, Poppy."

I feel the words spoken against the center of my chest. The rest of my clothes are removed slowly, his kisses continuing to flutter over my skin as it's revealed. Soon, we're both naked, and his cock is gliding into me. As my body grinds against his, he lets out a deep groan that makes my pussy spasm with want.

My mind blanks of everything except Keir and his touch. His body doing exactly what I needed. It's silencing all thoughts, focusing only on him and what he's doing to me.

This is all I need. *He* is all I need.

Twenty-four

Keir

I could lay here and watch her for hours. The weak morning sun casts a faint golden glow over her bare skin. Her hair is fanned over the pillow, and if I wasn't afraid she'd wake up, I'd be tempted to sift my fingers through it.

I could tell that Poppy had something on her mind for most of yesterday. Until then, she had been full of smiles. Something caused her to retreat into her head and as frustrating as it was, I forced myself to give her space. Time to work through it alone, even if it felt all kinds of wrong to do so.

Instead of getting her to talk about it, I did the only thing I knew how to do. I took her mind off it by worshiping every inch of her body. It was as if her thoughts simply melted away as I slid into her, her eyes growing soft as they cleared of any thoughts other than the two of us, in that moment.

Looking at the small clock on the bedside table, I stifle a groan. It's almost time for us to pack up and leave. Poppy has work to catch up on and I have meetings at the gym this afternoon.

Kissing my way along her shoulder, I really do groan when Poppy arches her back and pushes her ass into my already hard dick. We really don't have time for this, but there is no way I'm passing up the opportunity to be inside her, not if that's what she wants. Her hand snakes up and works its way into my hair, giving it a gentle tug. She shifts her leg over my thigh, and I dip down to line myself up at her opening. She's already so fucking wet, I can push in all the way, in one long thrust.

We quickly fall into a punishing rhythm. Fast and hard. The top of her body angles forward, away from me, and the change in position is enough to make us both moan. The sounds of skin meeting skin fill the room. Lifting her leg higher, I reach around to play with her clit. I won't last much longer and I need her to hurry up over that edge before me.

As if she knows, within seconds, she's fracturing apart, her groans muffled by a pillow. Her pussy contracts and it's like she's trying to pull my body inside of hers. I come on a strained roar, exploding inside her. As my vision blurs for a few seconds, I'm filled with images of her pregnant with my baby. I long for the day we can have that. It was something we used to talk about, us having a family. That dream has not changed for me.

As we both come back down to earth, three words escape my lips. They've been dying to get out, and the orgasm she just wrung from me has left me powerless to stop them this time.

"I love you."

I say the words out loud, for the first time in ten years. She's still for a second before her fingertips start running up and down my arm again, painfully slow.

"I know."

And then there is silence.

She doesn't say a single world after that.

Nothing falls from the swollen lips I just spent an hour worshiping. The three words I needed to hear most don't come.

The stillness of the room is suffocating, the silence only punctuated by quiet breaths and the deafening sound of my heart breaking all over again.

Poppy

I'm such a fuck up.

Hearing Keir say those words, the words I've been fighting to keep in myself, should have been a relief. I love him, and knowing he loves me too? That should have been enough to soothe my fears, but I can't stop the tumult of thoughts that keep assaulting me.

We stay there, both lost in our disappointment, until it's time for us to leave. Few words have been exchanged but despite the awkwardness, Keir has been his usual affectionate self. The same touches and kisses are still there, but I know he's confused about my reaction and probably regrets opening up like he did.

I hate myself for not saying it back to him.

In the truck, heading back home, it's quiet. As the miles tick by, I know I need to at least try and explain. I don't know what to say because I don't understand it myself. I love him, and I never want to be without him again, but Ted was right. I have a knot of fear that is holding me back. It's not that I think history will repeat itself, and it's not that I don't trust Keir. I don't think he would make that same mistake again.

It's me. I'm stuck in the past. Stuck in the memory of how it felt to be broken by him. The fear of going back to that dark place is what's holding me back. I'd had to fight so fucking hard to get out of there in one piece. My brain is telling me I'd be better off not even trying, that it would be easier to never have him back, if it means never losing him again.

Despite the silence reaching between us, Keir still holds onto my hand tightly. Like he's trying to anchor me in place.

I lack the courage to speak. By the time we make it back to my house, my nose is stinging as tears burn the backs of my eyes. When he twists the keys to shut the truck off, I can't look at him. What if he says he doesn't want to keep trying? His hand finds my chin, cupping my jaw ever so gently.

"Talk to me."

"I'm sorry."

"Baby"—his voice is hoarse with emotion—"never apologize for the way you feel."

His pained tone is enough to force the first few tears out of me. He's being so understanding and it's making this so much worse. With his fingers, he turns my face toward his. His eyes swirl with so many emotions as he continues.

“I want you. I love you and I want us to try again, more than anything. But I won’t force this. I’ll spend the rest of my life showing you I’m not that kid anymore, but you have to give me the green light. And you have to be sure it’s what you want too.”

My tears are now a torrent, running freely down my cheeks and covering his thumb as he still cups my face. I ache to tell him I'm sure. I'm sure that I want to try, that I want this as much as he does, but fear keeps my words locked inside.

“I don’t ever want you to feel scared or unsure. I don’t want you to ever feel powerless, not ever again, Poppy. I took something from you once before and I’m so fucking sorry.”

The sight of him, big and strong, and on the brink of tears, causes a rip to form in my heart. Knowing that it’s me doing this to him, causing his pain, is a killing me.

“I’ll give you space, but please know this isn’t me walking away. It’s me letting you make the choices you should have been able to make all those years ago.”

He gently pulls me closer, planting a featherlight kiss on my forehead before brushing away the tears that are falling so much harder now. “I love you. That won’t change, whether or not you decide you can do this with me or not. I love you, and I always will, baby girl.”

Hours later, I’m sitting on my favorite chair, overlooking my backyard.

I let him leave. Without saying a word to him. After he poured his heart out to me, he'd kissed me once again, before helping me out of the truck and into the house. He left me in my hallway with one final kiss. One more sweep of his lips over my tear-stained ones. Then he turned around and walked out, and I don't blame him one tiny bit.

Frank must sense I'm upset because he's not left my side, choosing to sit next to my chair all afternoon. I'm still stuck in my head when he jumps up and runs to the door, barking like crazy as he goes. My heart leaps into my throat. *Keir came back.*

I stand, frozen in place, as I wait for the knock. Instead, the door swings open, and a huge figure walks through.

When I see it's not Keir, my heart deflates.

Duke takes one look at my face, then drops the duffle he held over his shoulder and rushes toward me. His handsome face twisted in concern for me. Making it to me in a few large strides, he pulls me into a hug at the same time he growls out, "I'm going to fucking kill him this time."

Once Duke has moved us into the house, I tell him everything. How my emotions are running wild, how my fears are consuming me. He stays silent while I bleed my heart out to him. He's so quiet that by the time I'm done, I have no clue what he's thinking.

My tears have finally subsided, so Duke makes my favorite tea for me. When he comes back, he's still silent. That's my brother, he never wastes words. He's my silent pillar of strength. When he's ready to speak, he looks me dead in my eyes.

"His dad was right. You need to be sure you're all in, Pop."

This isn't news to me; this is why I'm here, crying all over myself.

"Tell me something I don't know already, Duke."

"Let me finish, little sis," he admonishes. "You got through it once, you'll get over him again, you know? If you decide not to give him the chance, that is."

Just the thought of not being with Keir is a white-hot lance of pain through my heart. I've always wanted him, even when I shouldn't have. When I thought I'd never be able to get past the pain, a part of me craved him.

"You will get over him. It will get better. Slowly, over time, you'll think about him less. You'll move on and someone else will take your heart. Well, they'll take most of it. I'm pretty sure that asshole will always keep a little bit of it. Just like I'm sure he'll always feel the missing part of his heart that you keep, whether you want it or not."

He's right, of course. I never got over Keir. That's why he will always have my heart. Not a just bit of it either—*all* of it.

"When did you get so wise about love?" I ask him. I don't think he's ever even been in a relationship. His dry laugh comforts me.

"Let's just worry about your relationship, instead of my lack of one for now."

"I love him, Duke. I don't want to be without him."

"Well, then go get him."

Whatever it was that was missing clicks into place. I love Keir. He loves me. We deserve our second chance, and I'm not going to stand in my own way any longer.

Giving Duke a watery smile and a kiss on the cheek, I quickly grab my keys before running out to my car.

Keir

Closing the door behind the last candidate, I turn back to my desk and throw my tired body down into my chair. I jam my hands into my hair and contemplate pulling it out, I'm that frustrated. Today has fucking dragged. After leaving Poppy at her house, I came straight here to start interviews to replace the trainer that TJ fucked and chucked. I swear, he better keep his junk away from the staff from now on.

Looking at the clock, I see it's already past five o'clock. I suppose I should be grateful these interviews have kept me busy all day. I've been able to keep thoughts of Poppy to a minimum. It didn't stop me checking my damn cell phone every ten minutes, though.

I know I promised her I'd give her space, *again*, but it goes against every instinct I have, to actually go through with it. I'm giving her two days before my ass is back on her doorstep to give her another reminder of why she needs to stop running from me. I'll keep giving those reminders for as long as she needs them.

I'm just about to start going back over the applications on my desk when Lucy steps in and takes the seat opposite me.

"What do you think?" she asks, motioning to the papers in front of me. Lucy sat in on the interviews with me and hopefully has the same ideas over who to hire.

"I'm pretty sure we'll go with Alex." I pull out the forms and pass them over to her, to remind her which one I'm talking about.

"Urgh, really?" She scrunches her face up as if she smells something bad.

"What?" The lady I picked out is more than qualified. "She seemed perfect to me." I lean forward onto my elbows.

"Yeah, I'm sure your brother will think so too," she scoffs quietly. Her eyes fly to mine when she realizes she said it out loud.

"So…you don't want her to work here because TJ might find her attractive?" I raise an eyebrow and wait for her to speak.

Her face is crimson and if I wasn't so damn frustrated, I might enjoy ribbing her over this. I've already worked out that she and TJ have some weird playground-style attraction to each other, but seeing her openly jealous is priceless. Lucy is usually unflappable.

"Employ who you want, see if I give a shit when she quits in a month."

She stomps out of the room and I go back to the applications. She might be jealous, but she also has a point. It might be better if we keep the pretty blondes away from my brother whenever possible.

A minute later, there's a light knock at my door. It's unusual for anyone to be here this late, especially anyone that would feel the need to knock. When I open the door, I'm surprised to find Morgen standing there.

"Hi, we don't have a meeting or anything today, do we?" I'm praying Lucy hasn't scheduled something last-minute and I've been too distracted to notice. Especially not with Morgen and her special brand of determination.

'Actually, I was just passing by and thought I'd drop off those samples we talked about. I won't be back out this way for a while. I'm headed out West for a bit."

Finally. Hopefully while she's gone, the drink company will get a new rep. One that won't try and get in my pants so often. Deciding to get this out of the way, I invite her inside, making sure to keep the door open so the guys still in the ring are in view. Another attempt at keeping her at a safe distance.

"Can I get you a drink or anything?"

"A water would be great. It's been a bitch of a day." She removes her jacket and makes herself comfortable in the chair. *Fuck, so much for getting out of here quickly.*

"So, what do you have for us?" I try to move things along without seeming like a dick.

She spends the next thirty minutes going through a bunch of products we've already talked about before today. She must think I'm stupid.

"Actually, I just remembered I have somewhere to be soon. Can I call in to the head office and get the rest of the info from them?"

I stand to show her to the door, moving to help with her jacket, but the next thing I know, she's throwing her arms around my neck and slamming her body against mine. Her lips make an attempt at landing on mine but thankfully, I manage to turn my head, so they barely touch my cheek. Unfortunately for me, the momentum of my head turn throws us off balance and we crash into my desk. Morgen's hands still gripping onto me for dear life, as mine try to push her back and away from me.

"What the fuck are you doing?"

"I know you want this as much as I do."

She's fucking psycho. She's also surprisingly strong, and her arms are not giving up on the hold they have on my neck.

"I see the way you look at me, Keir."

"I said stop, Morgen!"

I finally give her a hard push and she moves back just enough for me to break her hold on me. Before I get the chance to ask what the hell she is playing at, movement at the door catches my eye. My heart fucking crumbles when I see Poppy standing there, a look of horror on her face.

A look I've seen before.

"Tell me this is a joke?" She says it so quietly, I don't know if she's speaking to me or herself.

"It's not what it looks like, I swear to you." I take a step toward her, but she holds up her hand, as she's defending herself from me. I stop moving, scared she'll run if I keep going. "Poppy, listen to me. She's crazy. She threw herself at me, I swear to you."

Trying to keep my voice calm is almost impossible. When Morgen scoffs from beside me, I lose the tenuous grip I had on my patience. "Do not even fucking lie right now, Morgen," I seethe, turning to look at her.

If she ruins what little chance I had with Poppy, I will ruin her in return. By the time I turn back to where Poppy was standing, the doorway is empty.

"Fuck!"

I race around my desk to grab my keys so I can chase after her, but I'm stopped in my tracks when the door is kicked open wider. Poppy stands there, chest heaving in anger. She's so beautiful, even when she wants to rip my balls off. I don't notice until she pushes past me, to where Morgen is standing, that she has two sports bottles in her hands. I don't know who is the most shocked when she flips the lid off one and dumps the contents all over Morgen. The thick protein shake covers her face and upper body. Ignoring the screams of protest, Poppy yanks the lid off the second bottle and does the same. This time, the pink liquid gets dumped right over Morgen's head, splashing all over the floor.

"When *my* boyfriend tells you to stop, you stop," she grits out, as she pushes Morgen's coat into her sticky wet arms.

"Get out, before I see what else I can find out there."

Morgen doesn't look at either of us as she scurries out.

"Poppy, I promise—" I try yet again to explain before she gets a chance to turn her fury on me.

She shocks the shit of me when, instead of lashing out at me, she steps in front of me and looks at me with timid eyes. Where I expected to see hate, I see uncertainty.

"I'm the one that should be sorry."

"What the hell do you mean?" I'm getting fucking whiplash from all the crazy shit that's going on today.

"I was an idiot." She shrugs. "I let you walk away when I knew I should be holding on to you instead. I don't need time. I don't need space. All I need is for you to tell me you love me again. And that you forgive me."

Yanking her into my arms, I drop my head to rest against hers, my favorite place to be. Well, apart from being inside her, that is. I'm about to kiss her when she yanks my head to the side, eyes narrowing at my cheek.

"That bitch left her ugly lipstick on you." It's probably wrong, but I love that she's jealous.

"You know I would never, ever, do that to you again, right? Please tell me you know," I beg.

"I know. I think I've always known."

This time, she doesn't stop the kiss. It's a kiss filled with new beginnings. It's a kiss filled with love. It's filled with all the promises of how beautiful our future together is going to be.

"Say it again," I murmur against her lips.

"I love you, Keir."

Finally. That fractured part of me is soothed.

"Love you too, baby girl."

The most beautiful moment of my life so far is interrupted when my brother shoves his head inside and asks, "Why is Morgen outside in tears and looking like a drowned rat?"

Twenty-seven

Poppy

Six months later

Feeling the car come to a stop, I shift in my seat, nerves tickling at my belly.

"Can I take this off now?" I ask, reaching my hand up to the black satin mask covering my eyes.

"Stop it," Keir says, gently slapping my hand away. "Stay there, and I'll come and help you out."

I hear his door open, then close again with a *thump*. After a second, my own door opens, the warm evening air rushing in. Once I'm placed on my feet, I strain to hear any sound that will give me even a tiny clue about where we are. After driving for thirty minutes, most of which I'm sure was just to throw me off, I have no idea where we are. I can only hear the sounds of a passing car.

Keir takes my hand and moves us forward a few steps before I feel him stand in front of me. Lifting my hand, he places a gentle kiss on it, before moving it to rest over his heart. The wild thumps surprise me, causing my own to kick into a faster rate. He breaks the silence of the evening when he lets out a deep sigh.

"Do you remember our second first date that wasn't a *date* date?" Laughing at his description, I nod, surprised that I suddenly feel like I could cry. "Well, I kind of realized I never told you what my real plans for that night were, exactly."

The blindfold is removed; luckily, the evening light is gentle on my eyes. I blink away the darkness to see that we are standing outside of Addy's Book Nook. Instead of leading me away from there, like he did last time, he steps up and opens the door. The tiny bell above the door tinkles and just the sound of it makes me smile. I'd stayed away from here when I first moved home, my need to hide from Keir and all reminders of him more important than reconnecting with Addy.

Over the last few months, though, I've spent hours in here. We try to catch up at least once a week; most times, Diana will join us. Stepping further into the shop, I see that a blanket has been placed on the floor between two of the book shelves. There's a picnic basket and an ice bucket next to a pile of throw pillows, as well as battery-operated candles on some of the shelves. Some more are dotted around on the floor. There's music playing quietly from somewhere. It's beautiful.

Swallowing down the knot of emotion that creeps up again, I turn back to Keir. "You're right" —I nod— "this really is cheesy." The giggle I let out turns into a squeal as he yanks me against his body and tickles me. "Ok! Ok! I'm kidding, it's romantic!"

The laughter is stolen from my lips when he kisses me. "Oh, I'll show you romance, all right. Just you wait and see, baby girl," he drawls against my lips.

And show me romance, he does.

A little while later, after the food has been eaten and the wine almost finished, Keir pulls me to my feet and asks me to dance with him. With my head in its favorite place, against his neck, he moves us in time with the soft music.

"I could stay here forever," I murmur quietly.

"Speaking of forever, want to spend yours with me?"

My eyes fly to his as my hands move to cover my mouth. "Are you serious?" I gasp, as he drops to one knee right in front of me, holding my hands in his.

"Poppy, you walked into my life, and into my heart, all those years ago, like you were always meant to be there. Loving you isn't something I choose to do, it's something that is a part of me. A part of who I am." His throat bobs harshly before speaking again. "I made plenty of mistakes in my life, but you are the one thing I finally got right. I love you, and I want to spend every single day of our lives showing you just how much. Marry me?"

I can't speak past the tears as I nod at him. Of course I'll marry him.

He's my world. My safe place. My heart.

Epilogue

Keir

One year later

Why do I feel like this collar is choking me? And why is there is no fucking air in this stupid room?

My stare is drilling holes into the heavy wooden doors on the other side of the room. If they don't open soon, I'm likely to go down there and rip them off their fucking hinges.

She's late.

If I didn’t know her better, I’d say she was doing this on purpose, but that’s not my Poppy’s style.

TJ’s hand grips my shoulder and shakes me out of my thoughts.

“Do you think she’s changed her mind?” he jokes.

“I’m going to nail you in the balls if you don’t shut the fuck up.”

He chuckles to himself, getting a kick out annoying the fuck out of me.

"Chill. She's allowed to be late to her own wedding, dude. Loosen up before you scare all the guests away."

Taking a deep breath, I turn to him and return the squeeze to his shoulder. "I know I'm being ridiculous, but I'm still fucking amazed she said yes."

Before he can answer, the doors open.

They fucking open.

And there goes my ability to breathe.

I don't think I move a muscle as Elliott's two little girls make their way down the aisle, both holding tiny baskets of flowers.

"Hi, Uncle Keir!" Brooke belts out when she sees me, making all the guests laugh. Bailey just keeps chewing on her thumb as she quickly makes her way toward us. The girls take a seat near the front where their dad is waiting for them. I know how much it pained Poppy to invite the guy, but she'd do anything to support her best friend.

Next out is Lucy. When she gets close, I feel TJ tense beside me. He still won't admit what's going on with her, but anyone with eyes can see there is definitely something going on.

"Holy fuck," I hear him groan quietly when she stops opposite us. She and Poppy have become great friends in the last year, so it was no surprise when she asked her to be a bridesmaid today.

Last out is Elliott, walking with Duke. I can feel his hard stare. I know deep down he probably hates me, but he hides it well for his sister. I don't let it concern me. I'll just keep proving him wrong as long as he'll let me.

This is it. She should be here any second. I'm scared that if I so much as blink I'll miss something.

The music changes and the crowd go silent.

And then she's there.

I hear, but don't see everyone stand.

I hear my mother's gasp and small sob when she turns to see Poppy walking towards us with her arm tucked into my Dad's. The fact that he's walking her to me means so much to all of us, even he had shed a tear when she'd surprised us all by asking him.

Looking at her standing there with that beaming smile directed at my dad, I feel something I hadn't anticipated feeling today.

I feel a weight.

The weight of us.

Of every look, every smile and every touch we had ever shared.

I feel every wrong decision, every harsh word spoken and every tear she's ever shed because of me.

I felt every ounce of forgiveness she was brave enough to give me.

I felt every breath she took for us.

Looking down the aisle at her walking towards me, I see my entire world.

I take in the stunning gown that fits her like a dream, the long veil and huge bouquet of flowers in her hands, but I know if anyone were to ask me later, I'd never remember the details. Not when my memory would be filled with the expression on the most beautiful face I'd ever seen, the pure love and happiness that shone from her. Not when I could see my love reflected back at me ten fold. And as much as I would argue it, she had proved time and again she loved me, even when I fought it. Fought her.

I can't fight the tears that I swore I wouldn't cry, don't even attempt to. She deserves these tears. After every moment of pain I've given her, she's earned them.

When they finally make it to me, Poppy turns and gives him a hug. She quietly says something to him and when he moves back, he takes her face in his hands and kisses her on the cheeks.

'Thank you' he whispers it but I can still hear how thick with emotion his voice is.

Finally he places her hand in mine.

Finally, I'm not ever going to let it go. Not ever again.

Poppy

Resting my head against Keir's chest, I let him move us slowly to the song we chose for our first dance.

I can't believe today is real, that I'm finally married to Keir. Something I dreamt about for so long, but never thought would happen. The last year has been unbelievably amazing. When I gave up fighting it and let him, he made it his life's mission to make me happy. The best moment by far was when he dropped down on one knee and asked me to be his forever.

Our joined hands are clasped against his chest as the fingers on his other hand run gently up and down the lace covering my back. Every few seconds he kisses my hair. After a minute he moves his mouth close to my ear as asks "What did you say to my dad earlier?" I smile huge as I remember the look of joy on Ted's face.

Looking up at Keir I reply "I just said thank you to him and your mom, for raising a wonderful man. Thank you for loving me like a daughter" I reach up and kiss him gently once more "and I said that I hope you and I are half the parents they have been..." My heart races and tears make my voice too hoarse to speak. His eyes scan my face, looking concerned but he doesn't speak. Trying again I continue "I hope you and I are half the parents they have been to you and TJ when we have our own baby in about 7 months time"

"Really?" The word is barely even a whisper. We've stopped moving as he just stares at me. When all I can do is nod, he lifts me up and crushes me against him, before bringing his lips to mine for the sweetest kiss of my life.

We stay pressed together for another two songs, talking about our hopes and plans for the future. We discussed having kids, but finding out I was pregnant last week was a huge shock. As we move around the dance floor, I see Elliott seated at a table with the girls. There's no sign of Pete. Just as I'm about to go and see if she's ok, Duke walks over and says something to her. She gives him a tired smile then slips her hand into his. Before they go any further, he bends down and lifts Bailey into his arms. I'm shocked when she not only lets him, but actually buries her face against his neck. They move onto the dance floor and I watch as Duke pulls Elliott closer, Bailey still in his arms, and Brooke holding Elliott by the hand.

Before I can say a word, Keir puts his hand over my mouth.

"Leave them alone."

"But—"

"Leave. It." He laughs. "Let them figure it out."

He drops a kiss on my parted lips. I'll leave them alone.

For now, at least.

Keir

Seven months and four days later

Poppy's hand has mine in a death grip and I'm sure my hands are leaving ineradicable marks on her thigh. I'm fucking terrified. Any second now, Poppy is going to give birth to a tiny human. A human that we are going to be responsible for. One that we have to love, protect and somehow shape into a good person. Despite being in agony right now, she must sense my panic because she releases my hand and brings it up to my jaw instead.

Turning my head to her, I take her in. She's so beautiful it hurts to look at her sometimes. When she told me she wanted as natural a birth as possible, I flipped my lid. I wanted her in a hospital with every doctor and piece of medical equipment ever made. But because she has me wrapped around her little finger, I pretty much relented and we settled on a birthing center that had plenty of trained midwives and an on-call doctor if he was needed.

So here we are, her in a huge bathtub, seconds away from giving me a baby. A tiny part of her, of each of us. Her hair braided back, away from her face, has become dishevelled where I've been holding a damp cloth to her face, the small curls look like a halo. Stupidly fitting because she's always been an angel to me. Her eyes are tired and puffy from lack of sleep, and they're a sludgy brown that almost looks like chocolate, the darkest I've seen them since we've been back together. She's been adamant about not having any hard drugs and so far, she's only had some kind of gas that made her space out for a while. Now she's alert and ready to do this. Ready to grab parenthood by the balls.

Just like that, the fear eases and I know she won't let me fail. She'll be the balance I need, and I'll be the same for her. When the midwife tells her to push one last time, she lets go of my hand and reaches down into the water. I can't move as I see her lift a fucking baby up.

A baby.

My baby.

And just like that, the world stops.

Everything I'll ever need is here, right in front of me. If we have no more kids after this, or if she gives me ten more, I know I've got it all. I'll cherish this amazing woman with everything in me forever. I can't stop kissing her hair, her cheek, her neck. Anywhere I can reach. But the tears streaming down have me mute for a minute, and the multiple people in the room have faded away. The sharp cry the baby lets out brings the rest of the room back into focus. Poppy has it held close to her chest, and as I lean into her and place my chin on her opposite shoulder, the baby opens its eyes and looks straight at me. Everyone told me there would be a bond there immediately, but I didn't know it would feel like this.

"So Dad, you want to tell Mom what flavor you got?" the midwife asks, as she wipes the muck off the baby's head. Poppy shifts the arm supporting its bottom, and I gently lift the leg that's tucked up against its body.

"It's a boy," I whisper, while looking into my wife's eyes. "Thank you." The words are more whispers as I press my lips against hers.

She knows it's more than gratitude for giving me a precious son.

It's a "thank you for taking a chance on me and giving me the chance to score the ultimate prize."

The End

Acknowledgments

You know that saying, 'It takes a village to raise a baby'? Well in this case, it took a whole book community to raise this book baby. There are so many people I need to thank, so many people that made this possible. I know I'll forget people, so apologies in advance.

Adriana Locke, when you first shared that post asking for people to take part in the original Kindle World project, I didn't hesitate to sign up. The reason I didn't hesitate, was you. This story has been in my head for about two years, I never planned to do anything with it, trying to do it on my own felt too daunting. Your kindness, generosity and your belief that I could do this is what got me here. When the plan for this project changed drastically, you never wavered. You could have easily left the seven of us to deal

Mandi Beck, where do I start? Thank you for answering all of my stupid questions. Thank you for being my cheerleader. Thank you for helping me organise my vacation. I'd literally be lost without you (seriously, those Florida roads are no joke). Is it RARE time yet?

Tiffany Remy, have we worked out a way to clone you yet? I need a Tiff of my own. Thank you for everything you did for this project, I would have been lost without your help.

The Sensational Six –Lucy, Emma, Kristi, Crystal, Jenna & Jeanmarie.

We've been through some stuff haven't we? I couldn't have picked a better group of ladies to do this with. Thank you for everything.

Randy Fenoli - (Yes, the guy from Say Yes to the Dress.) These characters popped into my head while watching this one Sunday afternoon. The idea was suddenly there and I had no choice but to pick up my phone, open the notes app and write the epilogue. It was during another episode I wrote the prologue. After that they would not shut up. So, thank you, Randy, for inspiring me.

Kate, My Ace. I should write something epic here, same as you've done for me over the years, but you've always been better at words than me. Instead I'll just say thank you for being you. Thank you for turning up in my DM's that day. Thank you for being so weird. Thank you for being the best friend to me. I love you, please don't ever change.

Jo Webb & the rest of the FBBF Avengers – You ladies won't know this, but your signing has been a huge inspiration to me. Before the first FBBF, I'd only dreamed of being in the same room as some of my favourite authors. Your hard work and commitment to FBBF has given me the chance to meet so many people. Not just amazing authors, but bloggers and other fangirls too. Something else you gave me is confidence. You gave this painfully shy girl the opportunity to step outside of her comfort zone and make some real, lasting friendships.

Nicole Erard & Denae Mclennan, I can't explain how scary to is to share words you've written with other people. Thank you for reading this when it was little more than a vague outline of a story. Thank you both for helping me fill in all the gaps.

Monica Robinson, you are banned from reading this book so I don't know why I'm including you. Hopefully you never see it. If by some chance you do, thank you for not just your support, but your friendship too.

Sophie Broughton, I've said it before and I'll say it again. You are a star! Thank you for all the kindness you have shown me and this book.

Brenda Travers & Diane Hamilton, from the moment I posted about writing this book, you ladies have been there. You've shared and shared and shared. Thank you doesn't come close to conveying my gratitude.

Angela Hart, Karen Kay, Cornelia McAleese & Jen Raftery Ritter. You ladies have been in my corner since the very first time I posted about writing this book. You're always the first to like, comment or share my social media posts. I see it, and I appreciate it every single time.

Bailey Boughton, Lisa Ward & Morgen Frances – Thank you for letting me use your names. Bailey and Brooke will be such fun to write next. Morgen, you drew the short straw and had to be the baddy, sorry!

Melissa Pascoe, without you, there would still be no blurb for this book. Despite the fact that you and I had never had a conversation and you had never read a word of this book, you somehow managed to nail it in one try. You saved me from pulling all of my hair out in frustration. Thank you.

Bloggers & Bookstagrammers, I'm floored that any of you have signed up to support this book. I know first-hand how many new sign ups get sent your way every day. I know how time consuming it is. I also know how precious your time is and I'm eternally grateful that you'd use some of it help me out. Especially when there are so many phenomenal authors out there for you guys to support.

The Meet Me In Savannah reader group. When we launched that group, we had so little to share with you guys. We had no covers or blurbs. That didn't stop you guys from supporting us. Thank you for having faith that we would eventually give you books that were worth sticking around for.

A long time lover of all things romance, Emma Louise is a book blogger turned debut writer. She's a die hard bibliophile, addicted to tea (Real British tea) and speaks fluent sarcasm.

She lives with her husband, three children and overgrown puppy in South Wales, UK. Having been an avid reader for as long as she can remember, she's recently decided to try her hand at writing a love story of her own.

Goodreads: https://goo.gl/SV77Ks

Newsletter: https://goo.gl/7QAXcL

Instagram: https://goo.gl/Ac9Fng

Facebook: https://goo.gl/GwEYks

Reader group: https://goo.gl/vuiftL

Sneak peek…

Fixed

Coming late 2018

Prologue

Elliott

I shouldn't be watching this.

I should turn away.

I should close my eyes.

His hand gently cupping her face, their eyes connected.

I shouldn't watch him fist her hair, moving her head into the perfect position for his mouth to devour hers.

I should close my fucking eyes.

Instead, I watch him inching her skirt up her thighs. His fingers slipping into her underwear, her head thrown back in utter ecstasy. This is not for me to see. I should turn around and walk out the door.

The undeniable intimacy that floods the room around them is like a hot dagger to my chest.

The soft moans and muttered curse words ring in my ears.

I shouldn't be watching but there's no way I can stop myself. I need to know this is real, that my eyes aren't playing tricks on me.

I can't look away.

Not when she's my sister.

And he's my husband.

***

The warm evening rain soaks me as I blindly run to my car. Fumbling with my keys, I somehow drop my purse to the floor, watching through a fiery haze as the contents spill out, littering the concrete at my feet. My wallet bounces under the front wheel, landing open and showing my favorite picture of my husband and our daughters. His arms spread wide and he hugs them, one on each side of him. His hands squeezing their little bodies. His hands that were just touching another woman. Feeling like the world just tipped on its axis, I drop to my knees, not feeling the hard stones that dig into my bare skin. Ragged breaths rip from my body as I feel bile threatening to rise inside me.

I find my phone amongst the detritus and dial the one person that I know will get me through this. When Poppy answers after just two rings, the dam breaks. The scalding tears fall from my eyes in a torrent, choking me and stopping the words I desperately need to get out. I can hear her calling my name but nothing can break me from the nightmare I'm trapped in.

Nothing will take away the pain of seeing my life as I know it crumbles to nothing right in front of my eyes.

Printed in Poland
by Amazon Fulfillment
Poland Sp. z o.o., Wrocław

53449550R00122